I0535168

THE BANJO PLAYER

A SHERIDAN COUNTY MYSTERY

ERIN LARK MAPLES

The Banjo Player

A Sheridan County Mystery

Erin Lark Maples

LODESTAR
LITERARY

The Banjo Player

Book Five in The Sheridan County Mysteries series

by Erin Lark Maples

To Jane,
the perfect balance of judicial temperament and cheerleader

Prologue

Savageton, Wyoming, 1912

Two BOYS KNEEL NEAR a tin pail, their shins pressing into the rich brown earth. The same dirt smatters their clothing and dusts their cheeks. A dozen feet away, her hair teased by a summer breeze, their mother hangs linens on a clothesline. Soft, auburn curls brush her cheeks. She clamps clothespins between her teeth as she wrestles with the damp fabric.

"Why do we have to shuck the peas, Mama?" The older boy stuffs a pea pod, shell and all, into his mouth and chews. "Tastes fine whole," he says.

"Better for you that way," his mother says, exasperation crossing her brow. She glances at the rise above them.

The soft crest of the hill appears sharp from a distance. A few cows stray over the top, black figures against pale yellow grasses. Cloudless, the bright blue sky is oppressive, arching overhead.

The smaller boy frowns, causing his straw hat to fall forward over his brow. "I hate peas," he says with a pout and chucks one off into the dirt.

"Now, Mark, you say that about anything green. Peas are sweet. Good for you, too. Don't you want to grow up to be as strong as Big Mac?"

Big Mac is a neighboring rancher who tosses bales of hay like they were sticks of butter. Big Mac had helped with the calving that spring. Fixed the stall door. To the five year old, that made the man godlike. He pushes the hat back up and sighs. "Yes 'um."

Their mother turns back to the laundry, hanging first one sock and then its mate. "I've got an applesauce cake baking. Good boys who mind their mamas will get a slice after supper."

The older boy is quiet, thoughtful. He slides a thumb along the inside of a pod, popping each pea into the bowl. They hit the surface with soft pings.

"Mama?"

"Mmm?"

"Will Daddy be home for supper?"

Both boys watch their mother's shoulders stiffen. She pauses, mid-hang of a pair of patched trousers. Her jaw shifts, a brief acknowledgement of an unspoken pain. She gives herself a little shake and continues to clip the pant legs to the line.

"Your daddy will be home when the rail work's done, you know that."

"But Granger is so *far*," the youngest boy whines.

Hoofbeats thunder down the hillside, and three heads turn that direction.

A single rider heads their way. Sun glints off silvered pieces of tack. His kerchief whips behind him. The appaloosa is bulky and powerful, its legs a blur of movement.

He reaches the yard in front of the prairie house, and chickens scatter. He dismounts, reins in hand.

With a tip of his hat, he speaks. "Pardon me, ma'am. Might you be able to spare some water for a cowboy and his horse? It's fit to blazing out there. Old Thunder and I will be forever in your debt."

Their mother regards the man for a moment, one hand on her hip. He waits. The horse stamps a hoof.

Mark sees the man's spurs, braided lasso, and mile-wide grin. His brother sees the corner of his mother's mouth twitch upward.

"You may water your horse and refill your canteen, too. I have a pot of tea on the stove and can wrap a slice of cake for your journey."

Paul opens his mouth to protest sharing the cake, but his mother continues.

"But as this is a good, Christian house, you must leave those"—the boys' mother looks at the man's belt—"outside."

"Ma'am, I am forever in your debt." He unbuckles a leather strap from around his waist and deposits it on the stump they use for splitting logs. The man leads Thunder behind the house to where the family's bay roan has a small corral and shelter.

Mark thinks the man's teeth are white like hominy. His older brother wonders how the man knew where to put his horse.

"You boys stay outside," their mother says. "When you finish the peas, peel the potatoes. Paul, you keep an eye on your brother." She goes inside the house and closes the door.

Mark collapses backward in a gesture of protest. Dirt clouds puff up from beneath his little body.

Paul stares at the door. A steady hum of voices escapes the windows. He narrows his eyes, questions jostling for attention in his mind. When he hears his mother's laugh, he stands. After brushing off his pants, he moves toward the stump.

His father wears a belt. He and Mark use pieces of rope. Why would the stranger remove his, in the name of God?

When he gets near the stump, he sees why. Sees *them*.

The leather is tooled with oak leaves and acorns, a costly item. Its matching holsters hold a pair of silver pistols, each carved bone handle gleaming.

"Would you look at those," Mark whispers from behind his brother.

Paul startles, but before he can stop his little brother, Mark grabs one of the guns.

"Put that back," Paul says, a harsh whisper. "Mama said you're to mind me."

When he says her name, both boys look at the house. Paul thinks he hears some shuffling, a thump, and reddens.

Mark makes up his mind. "I'm Buffalo Bill, and I can out hunt and out ride any cowboy!" He whoops and takes off for the stand of cottonwoods that frame the water ditch.

Paul eyes the other gun, then his brother. The weight of decisions presses his cheeks like the afternoon sun. With another glance at the house, he reaches for the other gun and races off after his brother.

The boys scamper in the trees, pretending to aim, shoot, and die in a variety skit of their own making. They are so gleeful, so inventive, their shouts and play mask the sound of men on horseback until the riders are halfway down the ridge.

Mark aims his pistol at a reticent crow. "Say your prayers," he says and pauses for the bird's response.

In that moment, both boys hear the rumble as it nears. They look for the sound, feel its inertia. Paul presses Mark behind him with a hand to his little brother's chest.

A posse careens toward the small ranch house. Six riders atop their mounts, hats shading grim faces, head straight for their home.

Like a bullet, the stranger dives out the small rear window of the house. He doesn't see the boys.

With a timed leap, he is in his saddle and off, his clothes loose and flapping at his midsection. He makes a break for the rise, following the line of trees. Afternoon shadows stripe his escape.

A member of the posse shouts, then points in the direction of the stranger. The riders turn in one smooth bank of motion to follow the trail of dust kicked up by Thunder's hooves.

Gunshots ring out, their cracks shatter the still, thick air.

The boys, mouths open, look at each other, then at the weapons in their hands.

Paul's feet pound the earth as he runs for the shovel that leans in the shed. His body is all action, thought will come later. He takes Mark and they head for the fence line. He digs and digs. The hole must be big enough for their memory, too.

Beads of sweat stream into Paul's eyes. He runs back for the belt. When Paul picks it up, he rubs a finger across the design. Remembers the way the man looked at his mother. The way she looked at him.

Their mother weeps from inside the house. Paul considers handing over the pistols, then shakes his head. He will do her this favor. She carries too big a burden. He will be the man of the house now.

Mark is wordless when Paul returns, belt in hand, potatoes in the other. He watches his brother upend the potato sack, the tubers tumbling out onto the sparse grass. Paul holsters one pistol then holds out his hand for Mark's. Mark hands it over, bids his turn as a renegade goodbye. Paul holsters the second pistol and stuffs the belt into its burlap shroud. He drops the sack in the hole.

Paul and Mark look at the bag, limp and bulky in its grave. Mark wants to say a prayer. Atone. Paul shushes him and pushes dirt back into the hole.

Mark turns his back on his brother dumping shovelfuls of earth over the pistols. He catches a grasshopper.

Paul finishes filling the hole. He debates how to hide it. With his worn boots, he scuffs at the earth to blur the edges. Rain will help, but they are a month out from storms. Maybe two.

He wonders when they'll next check the fence lines for gaps. Maybe Big Mac will take him, teach Paul how to rewire and make the barbed tips. Then he will teach Mark next year if he needs help. Mark will be stronger, then.

Paul remembers turning six. His father gave him his very own knife. Taught him to whittle, strip leather, gut fish. He will give the knife to Mark. He will teach his brother.

Each night when they say their prayers, Mama asks God for news of their father. Paul thinks she should ask for their father back instead.

Their father sends letters, but Paul never reads them. He doesn't want to because they make his mother cry. Mama says the railroad will be finished any week now. Their father will return by train. She says this every time she reads a new letter, the worn paper creased and smudged from tears.

Paul stopped believing in the letters. He doesn't tell his mother this. Instead, he asks God for important things. Big things.

He will learn the everything else himself.

Paul scatters rocks over the site. Presses down on the surface. Erases the disturbance.

Mark releases the grasshopper and takes his brother's hand. From inside the house comes the scent of burning apples.

1

WITH A SWISH OF her hand across the gleaming bar top, Elizabeth wiped away the past and made fresh for the future. As she applied the damp towel to the resin-sealed surface of the wood, she marveled at the whorls and knots. Rings of time in the rich hues of gold and amber, streaked with darker tones. The live edge of the great walnut slab made for a unique focal piece of the brewery. *If only we could swipe our own slate clean with a wet rag and a little bleach water,* she thought.

A cooled strip of blue glass ran the center-length of the bar. This eye-catching feature kept beverages cool no matter the temperature. On summer days, it was a blessing of modern technology. On September afternoons, when the air teased frost, Elizabeth saw it as a reminder of the season to come.

She finished her task. Fresh coasters replaced soggy cardboard discs. Empty chip bags and used glasses were collected.

A couple from Spokane had stopped in. They were taking the long way to Deadwood. Stopped by for a few pints and an in-depth analysis of the woman's sister's taste in men. Elizabeth learned that for whomever this sister may be, Randy, Cliff, or Maddox were out of the picture. But Stephan, now he might be the one.

Elizabeth couldn't help but eavesdrop. This was an important skill for a waitress, bartender, or anyone who took care of customers. You could pinpoint when it was okay to interrupt to ask about refills or when to drop off the check. There were cues for when you should steer clear and come back.

Other times, you needed to know when someone needed help getting away from a too friendly date or if a cab was in order.

Listening in was an art form, one Elizabeth learned early. She'd listened around corners, from the backseat. On Tuesday afternoons and Sunday drives. When her parents fought late into the night, a glass hitting the wall, shattering. Shouts and tears. When her brother snuck out of the house through his window to go somewhere, anywhere but home. When it was safe to come down in the mornings to eat cereal and watch cartoons while the spent household slept in.

She thought again of her childhood as she restocked pint glasses. To many, childhood was a safe place for growing up, a card deck of memories one could take out and use to reminisce. For Elizabeth, the memories were scars. Long scabbed over, but still something she noticed and considered from time to time. How they had shaped her as an adult, decades after, was still becoming clear.

She bid the couple, recent empty-nesters, a safe trip when they left. The five-dollar tip was in her pocket, but it would stay with her in Sheridan County. Deadwood was on Elizabeth's must see list, among other stops in the Dakotas. Hoards of riders had come through on their way to Sturgis. Grabbed a beer before hitting the road again. She'd loved hearing about the haunting magic of the old town. Trips would have to wait, though. She had bigger goals in mind.

Elizabeth had won top prize at that summer's brewery festival. Her winning beer was a featured tap at Maximum. She hadn't known it would turn into a permanent placement. "For as long as you want it to be," Buzz said.

After the contest, Buzz had moved his whole operation to an industrial space off Broadway. An explosion of faulty plastic kegs had damaged the original brewery building. He had to move everything, kegs and all. Insurance and the endless cycle of repairmen made for a slow and steady rebuild. In the meantime, he made the best of the new spot.

On top of carrying Elizabeth's Pine Tip IPA, Buzz made her a job offer. He'd lost an employee when his son was convicted of tampering with a body. His other employees didn't have half the expertise of Elizabeth.

Buzz liked to say, "No one has taste buds until at least their thirties. You've got to be an adult for a decade or two before you know what's good and what's ditch water." Elizabeth told him she was a year short of thirty, and he claimed that God made exceptions for the exceptional.

Elizabeth considered his offer. He'd made it after her win and each month after. When school started again that fall, she considered it some more. She loved working with kids but had yet to regain the spark teaching once had. Brewing was a joy for her, chemistry that brought good cheer and the opportunity to create. But she couldn't give up the insurance, steady schedule, and summers off with her son.

In a temporary compromise, she accepted Buzz's offer with a catch. While her brother outfitted his barn into a new brewing space, she needed a temporary place to create. Elizabeth told Buzz she'd come in most Saturdays for a few hours if he'd let her use his brewing equipment.

Now, Elizabeth daydreamed that Maximum was her brewery. Buzz wanted to sell as soon as the remodel was complete. Retirement in a small beach town in Mexico was on the horizon. But Elizabeth had yet to save up for her own place, let alone a whole brewery. A home for herself and her two-year-old son, Rhett, had to come first. *I'll get there,* she promised herself.

When she finished wiping down the bar, she poured another round for a few regulars. Townsfolk hadn't minded the shift in location one bit. Sheridan was small, and they were loyal.

Buzz bustled in the back door, a sack of grain over one shoulder. "Thanks for waiting on me. I bought up 'bout everything they had left. Drive's killer on my knee. Trunk's full, though." He'd driven the two hours to Billings and back to pick up brewing supplies. They had plans for a pumpkin ale. "Still cheaper than shipping out here."

"I've got ten minutes," Elizabeth said. "You unload, I'll hold the door."

"Hot date?" At Buzz's mention of Elizabeth's love life, more than one patron looked up from their beers.

"You know Kade is in Denver this weekend." She'd started dating Kade Michaels, the owner of a local garage, that summer. The mechanic was at a trade show, and Elizabeth had a weekend to herself. *I wouldn't take him where I'm going today even if he was here.*

Buzz held up his hands. "An innocent question."

"He's giving the rest of us a bit of hope, that's all," Big Ricky called from his stool. A frequent customer, the mason was a friend to many.

"Right," Elizabeth said, a smile at the corner of her lips.

Buzz tapped at the register tablet to check sales for the day. Weekends stayed busy unless Wyoming snows made travel impossible. A typical September was mild, though the first snow could come through at any time. "Lunch rush?"

"We were slammed earlier," Elizabeth said. "Book club came in, followed by a big group of hunters. Couldn't have made for a funnier mash up."

The two groups had occupied opposite ends of the building. Orange vests and pixelated camouflage on one side, cowl-necked sweaters and notebooks on the other.

"Sounds like a middle school dance," Buzz said.

"You're not far off." Elizabeth removed her apron and hung it on a hook. She slid into her puffy vest, navy and purple stripes against emerald-green, and zipped it to her chin. Elizabeth slipped the skinny strap of her purse over her shoulder. She patted her pocket for her keys. "Manny wants a moment to check his set up, if you've got it," she added. "He said today's dry run went well."

In the new location, Buzz had room to park a few food carts in the lot. The brewery stocked chips, nuts, and other snacks, but Buzz knew more options were a good thing. Food carts gave his customers a reason to stick around and order more drinks. Manny Nuñez owned the newest cart, a hot dog stand.

"It shouldn't take more than a minute or two to get the rest of the load inside," Buzz said. "Back in a jiffy."

Elizabeth headed back behind the bar to wait. She eyed the place like a lioness observing her queendom. The bartop gleamed from her attention. It was a treasured piece from the old building. Buzz had hauled it into his temporary spot.

The rest of the place was rough hewn and patchy, but they'd worked to make it comfy, inviting. Buzz had built a hasty line of booths on one side of the bar and filled the rest of the space with tables. A plywood stage occupied a corner near the window. She'd lined it with a strip of cheap LED lights that looked great for evening shows. Buzz had sports memorabilia on the walls, and Elizabeth kept a front board full of fliers for events. Rustic, yes, but the result kept former customers coming back and brought new ones in.

Customers chose their favorite perch, cradled glasses in their hands. Big Ricky, one of the regulars, chatted with two of his buddies. The trio were midway through their second pints.

Connie Ann, a florist, occupied a booth with a friend. An abandoned plate of chips and salsa sat in front of them, two glasses of red ale close by. The florist leaned over her beer, its bubbles rising, while she listened to her companion. *Must be gossip*, Elizabeth thought.

A trio of women bookended the shuffleboard table. They wore bedazzled jeans and ponytails tucked into trucker hats. She heard Ricky mutter, "Buckle Bunnies" to his companions.

Hearty laughter broke out from a foursome in business attire who commanded a booth in the back. *Salesmen*, Elizabeth thought. One of the men called to a musician setting up on the small stage. The man fiddled with his guitar and amp while they chatted.

Another couple entered the doors. They removed their sunglasses and blinked in the dim light. The pair made their way across the pine floor to Elizabeth.

While they assessed the menu, Elizabeth's gaze strayed their way. The man wrapped an arm around the woman, and she leaned into him as they regarded the board hanging on the wall. Each was so comfortable with the other, like wearing a second skin.

They took their beers to a booth. Elizabeth watched them nestle together on the same side. They clinked glasses in a toast. The man said something and grinned, wider than the brim of his cowboy hat. The woman laughed, throwing her head back. They kissed.

In that moment, Elizabeth missed Kade. Was a booth in their future, somewhere? A place where they made it through the turbulence in their lives and achieved this level of comfort. Ease.

Another customer sidled up to the register, breaking Elizabeth's stare. "Sure smells like I'm in the right place," he said.

Elizabeth regarded the man, a moment of confusion crossing her brow. He was small, wiry, but with the energy of someone always up for a run, whether down the block or a marathon. *Military? Maybe.* Threads of white crossed his sable hair. His small dark eyes scrutinized the menu. He reminded her of a river otter, sleek, observant, and athletic.

"Welcome," she said. "What can I get you?"

The man studied the board behind her. A smile played at his lips as he scoped out their offerings. She caught a hint of cologne in the air and checked out his clothing. Polo shirt, pressed slacks. They sat well on a frame that had seen gym time.

If Kade had been there, he would have whispered two words to her. "Big Horn."

Big Horn was a small, but growing community. A host of the wealthy had begun to snap up land and plunk down mansions. They got a kick out of playing at being outdoor-types, bringing technology, noise, and demands from the cities. The benefit was an influx of jobs and tax revenue. The downsides, which were many, included outsiders sharing opinions where they weren't wanted.

To Elizabeth, this guy looked the part, but in the brewing business, his money was as good as anyone else's. "Can I help you find something you'll like?"

The man flashed a full-wattage smile. *Dentist,* Elizabeth thought. *Or a politician with veneers.*

"I'll take a porter. Please."

Project manager—or accountant? "Can do," she said, and took a glass from the rows laid out on the drying rack. "Been in before?"

The man slid onto one of the tall stools. "I'm new."

Bingo, Elizabeth thought. When she handed him the glass, she said, "Well, Maximum is the best place to get a beer, so you are starting off right."

He took a sip. A faint strip of foam lined his lip. He licked at it. "This is great."

"On the house," she said. "From one former newbie to another. It's a pretty special corner of the world we have here." Elizabeth glanced at her watch, then toward the back of the brewery. She'd need to get going, but Buzz had yet to surface.

"Thanks." He lifted the pint to Elizabeth, an appreciative gesture. "Used to work with some buddies out here," he said. "Business changed and I moved south. I always wanted to come back, and here I am."

Ranching? Nah. Oil? Too obvious. "I've fallen in love with it myself."

Big Ricky leaned over the empty space between himself and the newcomer to butt in. "If you ask me—"

"They didn't," the friend at his right quipped.

"Funny, Hal." Ricky shot his buddy a look and continued, waving his glass in the air. "We need to keep the lid on what we have going here. Too many people moving in. We'll become the next Sante Fe before you know it. Or San-An-Tonio. No offense, er...uh, mister." He raised his glass to Elizabeth. His companions tapped their glasses against his in solidarity.

"Don't pay him too much attention," Elizabeth said and raised an eyebrow at Ricky. The mason ducked her glare and turned back to his friends. "We all got here by someone moving someplace, whether this generation or a half dozen back."

The man smiled. "I can handle it. To be fair, I do care what happens here. You could say I've come back to...check in on business interests. Reinvest."

Venture capitalist? "Good to hear. I'm kind of new, and I've already fallen in love with the place," Elizabeth said. A year away from the city, the traffic, and her old life. She didn't regret a moment. "So, no shopping malls, okay?"

The man drew a finger across his chest in an X. "Scout's honor."

Buzz shuffled in from the back and over to the small, steel sink. He reached for the soap and flipped on the tap. "Where is my favorite co-brewer off to today?"

"Nothing big. An open house I wanted to check out." She'd seen the sign that week. The house was small—cozy, the advertisement said—but in a price range she could hope to afford.

Buzz's eyebrows shot up, two fuzzy, black caterpillars on his forehead. "Oh? Things okay with your brother? I guess I'd assumed if you moved out, it would be with a certain dark and swarthy mechanic—if he's lucky."

Elizabeth laughed. "Can't a gal want a house for herself?"

"Of course," Buzz said. "A house is a big step, that's all. Hope the place is what you're looking for."

"Me, too. See you all around." Buzz, Big Ricky, his friends, and the stranger lifted their glasses to her as she brushed past them with a wave.

Every step toward her old hatchback tingled. What was she doing, going to an open house? Buzz was right—looking to buy a house when she had a great place to live didn't make sense. What if she bought one and things with Kade got serious. Then what?

Still, it couldn't hurt to look, could it?

2

CHIPS OF RED SHALE crunched under the thinning tires of Elizabeth's hatchback. She wedged her car into a narrow, empty space in the crowded driveway. On one side there was a white sedan with an *I brake for martinis* sticker on the bumper. On the other side, a girthy cottonwood. She sucked in her stomach and squeezed out the door, careful not to ding the paint.

Streamers hung at the corners of an Open House sign that swung in the breeze. Voices filtered out of the house, signaling the gathering. Instead of heading inside, though, Elizabeth took to the little footpath toward the creek. The house flier formalized the yard at one acre of creekside property. A handful of towering pines, the solid, banked cottonwood, and a tiny cherry were the extent of the tree cover. Grass filled the spaces between but no more than a push mower could handle.

The house had been vacant since Elizabeth drove by on her first day at the little school in Story. Each day, her eyes would wander to the little cabin, curious. From the playground, she'd watch for signs of life, but there were none. Fall turned to winter, spring, summer, and then back to autumn. Now, she saw the place as a blank slate. Elizabeth pictured a couple of planters on the porch, each overflowing with petunias. A few solar pathway lights, a strand of party bulbs, a picnic table by the water. Tiny touches that would mean an inhabitant, the seasons, and a sense of home.

Sluicing water signaled the creek before she came to the bank. Piney Creek, controlled with locks and irrigation ditches, was a lion in some places, a lamb in others. Here, next to a small bridge, there was some life in the current, yet. Farther along, the four-foot drop to the waterline meant the bank, if there had been one, was long gone. Snowmelt, boulders, and a lack of grasses meant erosion.

A lone, sun-bleached plastic chair marked the viewpoint. Elizabeth sat. She pictured this spot as part of her morning routine. Coffee in hand, dog at her feet, rushing water. A person could get used to that.

Wouldn't be able to let Rhett outside by himself, she thought. At least not for a few more years. Casey's was wide open spaces, prairie grasses, and the watchful eye of Leia. There, Elizabeth could let Rhett play in the front yard. She watched him from the kitchen window. Here, a gushing body of water and a small highway with a blind curve meant adjustments.

Brushing off the back of her jeans, Elizabeth headed for the house. She took a deep breath at the door. *You're just looking*, she told herself. She didn't believe it, though. There was a solid kernel of hope, a *what if* that had taken root in her heart.

Elizabeth and Rhett had moved there on an invitation from her estranged brother with a car full of boxes and little else. Twelve months later, she had a full-time job, the beginnings of a catering business, and a savings account with a five-digit balance. But she doubted it was enough. At the moment, though, she had a house to check out. Details could come later.

You've got this, Liz. You deserve good things.

Casey had found a self-help book about business success. He played the audiobook at top volume each morning while he got ready in the bathroom. Elizabeth overheard the positive affirmations so often they'd leaked into her own conscience. But what could a little positivity hurt?

She'd saved for the opportunity to even consider buying a house. Scraped every penny together and combed online websites for loan options. The bank mailed an ad every other month. The text promised to help her buy a house, like the cute family pictured in front of their dream home.

Her best friend, Jo Wolf, said to get her feet wet, to go look at some houses, talk to a loan officer. Try on home ownership, see how that felt. "It's not for the faint of heart," Jo said, a bottle of cabernet between them. "Every time I fix something, the next thing breaks."

"But at least they're your broken things," Elizabeth said, and Jo laughed.

Elizabeth thought of her brave friend and reached for the doorknob.

Before she could push the door open, it opened away from her. Two women, giant sunglasses obscuring half their faces, pushed out. Each wore dark parkas, brassy hair twisted up in clips.

"It would be tight. Do you mind tight?"

"The agent said it could be two bedrooms with a partition. I could put one up when Beth and the kids come to visit."

"Or get one of those little guest cottages. You can order them online now. It would look cute out back."

"Not sure about that ceiling though..."

Elizabeth stepped into the house behind them. *The martini people*, she thought.

She'd entered an L-shaped living room and almost collided with a tall lamp. Its gold chain swung about, and she steadied the torchiere before moving on. One large window behind the worn sofa opened out toward the creek. Single-pane, she noted. Jo guessed the house was a fishing cabin, not set up for year-round use. She'd given Elizabeth a list of details to check, questions to ask.

Next to the living area was a small dining spot. A table for four filled the corner. Atop its surface was a stack of information sheets, a plate of cookies, and a business card holder. Elizabeth matched the woman pictured on the cards with the one commanding the back door in a peach suit. Her bangled wrist and bright pink lipstick matched Florida condominiums—not mountain cabins.

"As you can see," the woman explained to an older couple, "it's an efficient space. When you're cooking," she said, and pointed to the galley kitchen, "you can see the television. You're so close. Or you could take out this cabinet and open it up. And check out the bird feeder out back. Saw a blue jay out there this morning. Gorgeous songbirds to greet your day."

"Actually," Elizabeth said, overwhelmed by the crowd, "jays have quite the shriek. They aren't songbirds. They're corvids. Related to crows and ravens. They have other strengths, like intelligence."

The real estate agent's face smiled while her eyes narrowed at Elizabeth. "Welcome," she said. "Are you here to look at the house?"

Elizabeth nodded and reached for the folded sales flier she'd shoved in her back pocket. "I am. I have a few—a"

The woman turned her smile to the room. "Feel free to take a look around, then let me know if you have any questions. I'm taking offers today, and we have a motivated seller. I expect to get this tied up by the morning. We've got a hot property."

Elizabeth gave the woman a forced smile and turned away, eager to escape the withering glare. She ducked her head into the first doorway, a single bathroom. The tight space had ancient shower curtain rings and plain white tile. She'd known that anything in her price range would need some sprucing. There'd be a deep clean, a few trips to a thrift store for furniture, pots and pans. Her stomach gave a little flip, the pressure building.

Could she picture herself as the owner of a house? The idea was almost too foreign to hold, but she could feel it simmering at the back of her mind.

"There's a great window above the bath. High enough to keep you decent, but low enough to bring the outside in. Add a skylight and you'd be halfway to your own little spa in the woods." The agent ushered a woman with heavy framed glasses in Elizabeth's direction.

"What's that smell? It's earthy," the woman said. She wore a cream-colored sweater that screamed retired.

"Hmm?" The agent wasn't used to interruptions. "Oh, it's the woods, and the beauty of living inside a home made of the very thing that surrounds you. Like an extra layer of forest."

"So long as it isn't moldy."

To avoid the duo, Elizabeth slipped into the bedroom.

Advertised as a one bedroom with a bonus office, Elizabeth knew the place would be small. The office must be off the kitchen, she reasoned, a former mudroom. This was most definitely the bedroom.

The room was dark but sleek, outfitted with upgrades. A giant, queen-sized bed came up to Elizabeth's thighs. A remote on the bedside table could dial up comfort with heating and lifting options. A flat screen television occupied the bulk of one wall, a closet the other. The only picture in the room was an enlarged photograph of the Grand Tetons in black and white. A wall panel offered controls for the ceiling fan and lights. On either side of the bed were two end tables, one of which straddled a safe.

Elizabeth approached the closet, curious. With sliding wooden doors, it was larger than she'd anticipated. "This could be a plus." One side was open, the closed door obscuring some of the contents. She peered inside, curious.

While the room was modern, the items in the closet were anything but. On the top shelf, bowling trophies gleamed from within the dim confines. A row of musty bowling shirts, in tacky shades of orange and blue, hung from wire hangers. A handful of ties looped around the bar, and a selection of cowboy boots slumped below the clothes. A fishing pole leaned against the back wall. Elizabeth would have to tell Jo her guess was correct. This closet held the history of the place, its owners' stories.

Elizabeth wanted a place to put her own memories and knick knacks. A shelf for Rhett's trophies, his school pictures in frames on the wall. With a few touches, this place could work for them. Maybe she would learn to fish and then teach Rhett. This place felt right, like she was meant to be there.

She needed to call the agent Jo had recommended. Come back for a personal tour and get her questions answered. She wouldn't bother asking the lipsticked professional in the living room. Elizabeth needed to contact the bank and go over her budget one more time.

This place had graduated to a desired possibility.

Now, how to get out, get the information she needed, and make an offer in time. A small door opened to the outside from the bedroom. Elizabeth opened the door, half hoping for a quick escape.

Instead, she found a tiny sleeping porch, no bigger than the size of a cot. Screened walls and a solid roof meant the best of the outdoors. Warm nights under the stars without the threat of rain or mosquitos.

She could see Rhett falling in love with this space, a boy who was happiest outside. His newest speech therapist liked to hold his sessions outside when they could manage it. Her ex and Rhett's father, Nick, had found the woman after an extensive search. He paid the extra fee for her to drive over from Gillette, and Elizabeth was grateful. Watching the woman work, it was clear she knew her stuff.

From her spot on the little porch, Elizabeth heard someone enter the bedroom. She panicked. How to get out? The porch had a padlocked door to the yard, a missed detail on the part of the realtor. She pictured the woman cornering her on the porch. She'd demand to see her bank statement and deny her offer on the spot.

Instead of heels clacking across the floor, though, Elizabeth heard a different sound. A shuffle and a grunt, followed by the *plink, plink, plunk* of a stringed instrument—one in need of tuning. She peeked into the room and saw a man sitting on the bed, his back to her, a banjo resting on his lap.

The case yawned open on the bed. He shook back his curly, salt and pepper hair and broke into a twangy version of *Man of Constant Sorrow*.

Elizabeth recognized the tune from her single date with Justin almost a year ago. The Occidental, the chicken fried steak, the warmth of a room filled with musicians and their fans. A trio of cowboys crooned into a microphone while their fingers plucked the strings. The song struck one of her heart strings, a pinch point of nostalgia she was never going to shake. Songs could do that, transport you through space and time in a blink.

The man picked a few more notes, and a string snapped. He cursed under his breath before setting the instrument back in its case. He stood up to reach into the closet.

Elizabeth frowned. She knew open houses were an invitation of sorts. Peering into a cupboard or two and taking a quick stock of the medicine cabinet were all part of the territory. Digging into belongings and playing them reached a new level. A violation of some social code. While she watched, he slid a leather-wrapped, flat box out from deep in the back. He brushed a hand across its surface, sending dust bunnies into the afternoon light. When he lifted the lid, Elizabeth glimpsed a carved bone handle and a silver barrel.

To her horror, Elizabeth sneezed. A reaction she regretted the moment her nose began to tickle from the dust. The man snapped the box shut and glared in her direction. His eyes were dark, the sneer at his cheeks a menacing challenge.

"Who's there?"

"I liked your playing," Elizabeth said, peeking out from the porch, her voice a half-whisper. "Did you know banjos are over 400 years old?"

Four full beats passed. The man stared at Elizabeth, and Elizabeth willed a smile to stay on her face. One of them terrified, the other thoughtful, as though chewing on the moment. A decision.

Mind made up, the man slid the box back into the depths of the closet. He stomped out of the room, and Elizabeth exhaled the breath she'd held.

He continued down the hall, and she heard him over the din of voices. "That's it," he hollered. "Everyone out!"

3

WITHOUT A BACKWARD GLANCE, the man had left the bedroom, and Elizabeth, to iterate his message.

"Get out. All of you." His was a voice used to quick response. An executive, a boss.

Elizabeth skittered back into the bedroom. She was careful to close the door to the sleeping porch behind her. Unsure of how to exit but without a better option, she made her way back toward the living room.

In the main area, the man stood toe-to-toe with the realtor. She, in her beach tones and perfume, was in stark contrast to his dark denim and bearded face. Attendees clucked around the pair like chickens.

"I'll say it one more time. Get. Out." He spoke through his teeth, quiet yet venomous.

"I don't know who you are, but this is an open house. I am the realtor in charge of the event. Unless you are about to make an offer on the place, I'm going to call the police and have you removed."

When the man laughed in response, the realtor wilted in her heels, a subtle shift of her body weight. "Go ahead," he said, challenge shining in his eyes. "I'm not worried about them."

The woman fumed, her hands in fists. The remaining shoppers ringed the duo, watching. Some had phones out, no doubt sending "Guess what?" texts. Elizabeth eyed the front and back doors. Neither was accessible without brushing past one of the combatants.

"I am a professional," the realtor said. Her words held intent, yet her voice wavered. "I was hired to sell this house, which until you arrived, was going well. I've already had two offers and expect three more tonight."

Damn, Elizabeth thought. How could she hope to compete? She hadn't considered the potential for a bidding war. Her heart sank.

"If you want to get in on this place, I suggest you make an offer. Through your own agent. My job is to get the best package I can for my client, not give in to someone who uses threats as a strategy."

"Who exactly is your client? Look, lady, I don't care who you are or what you think was going to happen here. I'm telling you, in no uncertain terms, that if you don't get out of my house, I'll be calling the sheriff. I'll be reporting how unprofessional you are to them, whatever board holds your license, and anyone else in this town who will listen." The man was huffing now. His chest heaved, sweat across his brow.

Without another word, the woman grabbed for her purse, muttering. She dug out a cell phone and tapped at the screen. She wedged the phone under her arm before gathering her belongings from the table.

"Go," the man said to the onlookers. "You, too. *Get out.* Go spread your gossip. I know you're itching to do it." He held up his hands, each in a fist. "See? The shackles are off. Now get off my property before I turn you all in for trespassing."

The half dozen people who'd stayed to watch the confrontation left, whispering to each other. The real estate agent handed her card to a couple and mouthed, "Call me." With a warning glare from the man, she pocketed the rest before ducking out the front door.

Elizabeth had tried to scoot around the man, but his bulk blocked the tiny hallway. With the crowd gone, he ran his hands through his hair and turned to assess their wake. She darted out and put her hand on the front doorknob to yank it open. It wouldn't budge. The man watched, the corner of his mouth curled up while she struggled. When the door gave way, she turned to him. "Over half the population doesn't know how to handle an embarrassing situation. I wouldn't take this personally."

The fire within burned out, the man was a dragon after the attack. With a snort and a quick nod, he crossed his arms.

Before she ducked out the door, Elizabeth added, "I really did like your playing," and bolted.

4

ANGRY WORDS RANG THROUGH Elizabeth's head the handful of miles it took her to get to Rhett, to hug him tight.

They weren't the words of the stranger, though. The bear of a man who'd raged in the tiny cabin had terrified all, including the overzealous agent. He was a man whose command of the situation seemed both absolute and questionable in the same breath. Elizabeth would consider that event in time. First, she had to shake her own past.

When the yelling began, Elizabeth was her eight-year-old self again. Crouched, face pressed between railings with a stuffed bunny jammed under her arm. The little girl who huddled on the landing while a war raged in the kitchen. Bottles would smash and the fight would end in an abrupt and sickening silence.

To distract, to cope, to survive, young Elizabeth developed a habit. She read their four condensed encyclopedia volumes, night after night. Her mother had scored them at a yard sale and added them to the scant number of books in their house. Elizabeth read them, though. She could almost lose herself in the pages, forget the chaos around her and visit the exciting, the exotic. Delving deep into facts, she comforted herself with the wide world around her. Outside the house, life was different.

In reflex, each moment the shouts and screams sounded in her mind, a stream of facts burst in.

"I never should have married you. You are useless. A leech!"

"And you are nothing but a drunk!"

The bumblebee bat is the world's smallest mammal.
"I work all day to return to a sad mess of a woman."
"You used to have potential, to want a real life. Now look at you. Nothing but trash!"
Africa extends into all four hemispheres.
"You are an ugly, aging, beast of a woman!"
It takes a drop of water ninety days to travel the Mississippi river.
"I hate you!"

Elizabeth spent her drive trying to expel the voices. The stress must have painted her face as Jo said nothing the first few moments after Elizabeth arrived. The woman recognized ache and need when it came to her door. She would make way for emotion.

Jo, wife of Sheriff Wolf, was the amateur caseworker for half the county. Many nights, the coffee pot stayed hot as Jo did her best to console, counsel, and comfort. She considered it her duty to keep people out of her husband's patrol car whenever possible.

At this moment, Jo saw a mother clutching her child for comfort and waited. She stooped to scratch the heads of her two golden retrievers. They crowded the doorway to greet the visitor. In contrast, Leia, Elizabeth's Chinook dog, remained on the doormat. She gnawed at an antler chew toy, awaiting departure.

"Have time for a cup? It's lukewarm, but I got some of that fancy creamer. We can put it over ice and pretend we're in Europe," Jo said.

Elizabeth lifted her face from Rhett's shoulder. Tears streaked mascara across her cheeks. She sniffed. "An afternoon in Paris sounds pretty magical right now."

Jo headed for the kitchen and fished out two glasses from a cabinet. Ice clinked against the glassware as Jo busied herself with the drinks.

Elizabeth followed behind with Rhett. In the kitchen, he wiggled, a universal request to get down. When she set him by the table, he joined the pile of dogs in the living room. He offered the golden retrievers first one toy and then another. "Two," he said to the goldens.

"That's this new therapist," Elizabeth said. "Numbers are the new focus."

"Oh?" Jo brought two glasses to the table. She inserted a table knife in one and then the other and stirred, integrating the creamer with the coffee. "Voila. Iced something-or-other. Now if only we could get a decent croissant out here. I blame the elevation."

"Yup. Ever since she switched to meeting us at the ranch for his sessions," she said, and took a sip. "This *is* good."

"I know. You don't want to see how much sugar is in it. It's oat-based, though, and doesn't that count for something?"

Elizabeth nodded and took a second sip. "The first therapist was nice enough, but Rhett didn't connect with him at all. I feel bad, you know? Like if we'd thought to go outside it might have worked with him. Anyway, with this lady, it's almost like Rhett is there to entertain her."

"How so?"

"He gives her a tour, in a way. Points out the animals, tells her their names. She'll ask questions, suggest a word, string others together...it feels natural for them."

Jo spun her glass on the table top with two fingers, a slow turn. "Like getting a massage outside in Hawaii?"

Elizabeth laughed. "I would assume so. Never been."

"Clint took me for our twentieth. Piña coladas, luaus, gorgeous beaches...come to think of it, we don't yet have plans for our twenty-sixth..."

"Should I slip him a hint?" This was why Elizabeth was grateful for Jo. Five minutes with her friend and the weight on her shoulders was lighter already. Manageable, once again.

Jo grinned. "Maybe I'll make his favorite, elk meatloaf, and see what happens from there." She took another sip and looked at Elizabeth. "Glad the new therapist is working out. How was the open house?"

Elizabeth blinked back a lingering tear. "The house was fine, but it isn't for sale. There was a—mix-up. Or something. Anyway, the whole way back here, I got stuck thinking about my parents, and it all hit me. I don't know if you can ever escape your childhood."

"That's a big leap for our Parisian afternoon. I'm going to need a few more details."

Elizabeth told Jo about the open house and the return of its owner.

"Wait, which house did you say it was? The little yellow one?"

"No, the log one by the bridge. With the carport. Do you know the guy?"

Jo's brow pinched at the center. She'd tucked a few wavy strands of hair behind her ears, thinking. "Maybe...it's been a while. Not sure if it's changed hands in the last twenty years. I'll ask around." Her face took on a distant look. She turned her gaze toward the window. "In other news, I'm trying a new recipe tomorrow night. Pad Thai. You all coming?"

Elizabeth didn't miss the change of subject. "Not sure about Danny, but I know Casey will be here." They'd developed a habit of Sunday Suppers together. Occasionally the Blau siblings would host. More often than not, they'd eat at the Wolfs'—especially if Clint was working and it was Jo alone in the house. "What should I bring?"

"Papaya salad."

"How do I make that?"

"With papayas, I assume. Not *too* spicy, please. I've heard it's amazing. See you at six?"

"If I can avoid any other awkward encounters with enraged mountain men, I'll be there."

5

"I GOT T-SHIRTS!" CASEY called to Elizabeth the moment she and Rhett stepped through the door. From the couch, her brother held up a shirt in front of his face. "Aren't they great?"

Across the back of a navy T-shirt were the words Blau Brewing in a bold font. The Bs were larger, offset, so they linked together. Casey flipped the shirt to show her the double Bs over the left side of the front.

"Don't you love it?"

Elizabeth handed Rhett a dog biscuit from a jar to offer to Leia.

"Good dog," the boy said. The small interaction bought her time to decompress from her earlier thoughts. She plastered on a smile and faced her eager brother.

"They're awesome. I guess I thought they would be something we'd design together."

"You hate them." Casey's hands fell to his lap, a pout on his lips.

"No, I like them. I do. They're great. The logo is great. The color makes sense." Elizabeth watched her brother frown at the box of shirts on the table. "For real. I'm sorry, I—" She trailed off.

"I can take it," Casey said. "I'm a big boy. I'll send them back. Cancel the koozies."

"Koozies?" Elizabeth plucked one of the many throw pillows from the couch, clutched it to her chest, and fell into its spot. Casey had one of the comfiest and most decorated sofas in the county. Elizabeth laid her cheek against the plush gray-and-oatmeal-striped fabric. "I'm distracted, that's all. I had a makeshift therapy moment at Jo's, and I'm still a little raw. The shirts are great, promise."

Casey's eyes met hers. He thumbed through the T-shirts in the box and draped one over her knees. "Risotto and pinot gris. Quick as a wink." He turned to fluff the pillow against which he'd sat—a tug on opposite corners followed by a chop to the top edge—and headed for the kitchen. "If we're going to get into ancient history, let it be over a decent meal."

While her brother, a gourmet in his own right, finished the risotto on the stove, Elizabeth sat cross-legged with Rhett. Her son had constructed a castle from blocks. He then stacked animals at the top of each tower. An orca, a rooster, and two wolves stood sentry at the corners. Her role was to add another tower.

"Definitely fortified," she said to Rhett. She thought about her own desire for a house to call her own, a place to make safe and strong. "Anyone else need to live here?"

He blinked, thoughtful, before adding an elephant figurine. "Phant," he said, as if confirming the assignment.

After dishing out the food, Casey uncorked a bottle and poured, the unofficial signal that it was time to eat. Elizabeth paraded Rhett into the bathroom to wash their hands. Together they then joined Casey at the island where steaming plates awaited them.

"This smells amazing. Mushroom?"

"Freeze-dried chanterelles."

"Peas," Rhett said, holding up one of the bright green spheres.

"And peas," Casey said. That week's homework from Rhett's therapist was mirroring good word choice. Elizabeth had waited a year longer than most mothers to hear her child's first word. It was hard to break her habit of astonishment and praise, but to Casey that came easy. Casey folded the practice right into his duties as uncle. "From the farmer's market," he told Rhett. "Chickens love them. I know it's a typical spring crop, but early fall works, too."

Elizabeth held up one of her own peas to match Rhett's. "I love peas. Bright green. And Jo may have a line on some fresh mushrooms."

Casey took a sip from his oversized goblet. "Now, can you tell me what had you crumpled like silk on a humid day? Or is this one of those times when we wait for junior to go to bed?"

With one hand on the stem of her own glass, Elizabeth glanced at Rhett. With a child who spoke much less than his peers, it was easy to forget he listened to everything they said. The speech therapist said that was a common mistake parents made. Elizabeth would be careful.

"It started when I went to an open house for a house that isn't for sale." She explained the explosive homecoming. Casey made a face like Jo's as Elizabeth described the house. "Do you know the guy?"

"Not a client, but it's possible. I don't know as many people in Story."

Elizabeth continued, moving to the memories of their past. She wouldn't give details in front of Rhett, but she didn't need to. Casey had been there. He knew what it was like. "It's like I found myself drawn right back into the past. Back home. I don't want that for Rhett, not ever."

Casey set down his fork. He put a hand on her forearm. "That won't happen. Even if you lose your mind and run off to join the circus, I'm here. We won't let that happen."

Elizabeth began to tear up again. "But Nick...back then. What if..." She squeezed her eyes shut against the tears. A few slipped out.

Casey passed her a tissue. He distracted Rhett with a picture of a hawk on a telephone pole while Elizabeth collected herself.

Her brother knew she blamed herself—and Nick—for Rhett's speech delay.

While she could never prove it, she'd read enough. No amount of protests from Casey, Jo, or anyone else could convince her otherwise. For the first year and a half of Rhett's life, she and Nick had fought about almost everything. His cheating, her career. Family. Never physical, but absolutely a verbal assault on the senses. Elizabeth was certain the anger and volume had an effect on the baby down the hall. It had taken all her courage and what few resources she had to end the marriage, end the fighting. It was the right choice. She and Nick were on a path to healing, and this could only help Rhett. Still, Elizabeth prayed every night for the ability to erase her past failures. To be the mother Rhett had always deserved.

When she'd taken another sip, Casey spoke. "I'll say it again. You two are welcome here as long as and whenever you like. Forever. You and I will *never* allow the places we call home to turn into that nightmare."

"I know," Elizabeth said. She was grateful for her brother. Grateful for the chance to rebuild their sense of family. "It's just that—"

"And it's okay, too," Casey continued, "if you decide to move out some day. Especially as that bear-sized boyfriend of yours would make this place a tight fit."

"Kade is no taller than Danny," she teased.

"Truth. The point is, I remember when I got my freedom. It was intoxicating. I didn't want to rely on anyone ever again. I didn't think I could, so why plan for it?"

"I know, I know. We all need each other. It's what makes us human."

Casey shook his head. "It's not that, though that kind of unicorns and rainbow stuff is legit. I've got a lot of plans with my little ranch hand here." Casey slid a bowl of blackberries toward Rhett. "It's the running, Liz. That's what will get you in the end. It's pointless. We can try to escape the ugly parts of our past, but it won't work." He turned back to her, his jaw tight. "It comes with you, you know, in the moving boxes. The pain."

Elizabeth looked at her brother, and her lip trembled. He'd been the first to leave. Had survived—escaped—the longest. How much had he suffered in the years between his escape and now?

Casey shoveled up another forkful of steaming risotto and reached for his glass. "You don't get to leave the past behind. But you do get to decide whether to unpack or leave that junk in the attic."

6

MOTION LIGHTS IN THE driveway flickered on. Elizabeth's attention snapped to the windows and the growing twilight.

"Kade's truck," Casey said. "He didn't text you?"

Elizabeth pulled out her phone. A quick flick on the screen revealed the missed messages confirming that he'd be by tonight.

"He did. I didn't see them."

"I didn't think it would be a problem," Casey said. "He wanted to talk plans."

Elizabeth spotted design books, sketch paper, and Casey's prized drafting pencils on the kitchen island. "It's not," she said. She heard the slam of a truck door and boots on the deck. "Even if we weren't, well..."

She hadn't—no, couldn't—tell her brother that she and Kade hadn't taken their relationship that far. Yet. Elizabeth admitted that she had trust issues. Could still remember the smell of Nick's conquests on his shirts. The shame of meeting the women—his assistant, her hair stylist, the mail carrier—and finding out they'd slept with her husband was too much to bear. When things got hot and heavy with Kade, she'd been the one to pump the brakes. Said she needed to take things slow.

He'd been understanding. Respectful. Patient.

Kade had his own past to reckon with. His father's employees had attempted to leverage Kade in their shady dealings. While Kade couldn't prove his father had anything to do it, he couldn't clear the man from guilt, either. He became the guardian for his sister's son, Benny, while his sister spent the next decade in prison. His family drama could make anyone's head spin.

As a couple, they still danced around each other's backstory. Each also had a child with specific needs at the center of their home life. Elizabeth had her son, Rhett, and Kade had Benny. If the average relationship was complicated, theirs was a rocket ship schematic.

A knock on the door signaled Kade's arrival. Casey lifted an eyebrow to signal he was waiting for her to finish her thought before he opened the door.

"Of course I want him here," she said, the words tumbling out. "I was only saying that even if he and I weren't together, it's your house, and—"

Casey flung open the door and extended his hand before she could finish. Kade clasped Casey's hand in his own. Coppery with a slew of tiny scars across the skin from various mishaps at the garage, Elizabeth loved Kade's hands. They were like the rest of him, strong and capable.

"Come on in. Timing is perfect. We were just talking about Liz's day."

Elizabeth frowned and drew her hand across her neck. It was a frantic gesture to quiet her brother's loud mouth.

"Oh?" Kade turned his warm smile and golden eyes her way. "I'd love to hear about that myself." He had a handful of papers under one arm. One was a set of blueprints. He paused near Rhett in greeting. "Hey, little man, how goes the farm?"

Casey either didn't see or outright ignored Elizabeth's silent pleas. He continued his trajectory. "She went to an open house in Story."

Brothers, thought Elizabeth, and shot him daggers with her eyes.

Kade's back was to the Blau siblings, but Elizabeth saw his shoulders stiffen. "Oh, really?"

Crud. Casey didn't know that last week Kade mentioned wanting her brother's help. He planned to transform the farmhouse he'd purchased into a real home. A family home. Elizabeth hadn't known what to say. She hadn't been ready to explain all the reasons she needed independence right now, not commitment. Needed to make her own way first. She'd commented that remodels always seemed to take longer than anyone planned, but her brother was the best in the county and left it at that. When Kade changed the subject, Elizabeth bit her lip and looked away, guilty. From his reaction to Casey's comments, she knew Kade hadn't forgotten their conversation.

Casey fanned out his books and portfolios across the island. "Yup. She said the whole thing turned into something out of reality TV. The owner showed up in the middle, kicked everyone out. Said the place wasn't for sale. Sweet spot, too. Can't blame the guy. Crick-side. Great access to the mountain. Can I get you a beer before we take a look at some swatches?"

Elizabeth attempted to take the reins in the conversation, steer the topic elsewhere. "I'm working on a pumpkin ale with Buzz. There's a batch in the kegerator. We're getting close to something good. You can tell me what you think."

Kade wasn't listening. "Where did you say this place was?" The crows' feet at the corners of his eyes deepened. He laid a palm on Casey's books but didn't look at the page.

"Story," Casey answered, liberating a couple of glasses from a shelf. "That place across from the school. The fishing cabin, right, Liz? Would have made a great commute for you."

"The one with the metal roof?" Kade's face was pale, ashen, his voice stern, probing. He volleyed his attention from Casey to Elizabeth, seeking answers. "Carport out front. Circle driveway?"

Casey looked to Elizabeth. She nodded.

"Dammit," Kade swore. "I need to make a phone call."

7

FROM HER POSITION AT playground duty Monday morning, Elizabeth couldn't help but watch the house.

The night before had fizzled before it had begun. Kade made his phone call out by the barn. Through the window, Elizabeth watched him pace a line through the soft earth, the phone pressed to his ear. After ending the call, he stood in the yard a few minutes longer, staring out into the dark. When he returned inside, he asked Casey for a raincheck, planted a kiss on Elizabeth's cheek, and disappeared into the night.

She'd sent him a text that morning. *Miss you. Call me?* He replied that she could count on it.

Now, she chewed on his reaction to the arrival of the man across the street.

The usual crowd gathered in the staff lounge. They circled the Formica-topped table wedged into what passed for a break room. An ancient refrigerator, a small bank of lockers, and the massive, temperamental copier completed the room.

Elizabeth's co-workers conducted their predictable pattern of conversation. It was a song she could play by ear.

"I made this new recipe last night. Asked for smoked paprika but we only had regular, so I..."

"Rachel's mother wore a bikini again for drop off. Does she own a calendar?"

"Scores are down again. How long until Ridenour is on our backs?"

Elizabeth had looked down at her half-eaten sandwich, dry and lackluster, then up at the clock on the wall. Twenty minutes left.

"I think I'll get some air," she said to the room. The buzzing paused for a beat, then the hum resumed in her wake. She tossed the remains of her meal in her lunch bag and pushed her way outside.

The Story School, a newer, four-classroom structure, settled into a curve of road that wound through the small town. Elizabeth paused at the edge of the brief parking lot, looked both ways, and crossed the street.

The house was quiet. The slim bathroom window was open, and a swath of fabric flung over the casement. In the carport, the front door was propped open, the screen door in place. A broom and dustpan leaned against the wall.

From within, Elizabeth heard whistling. *Yankee Doodle*, she thought. Before she could second-guess her motives, she rapped her knuckles on the open door. The whistling stopped.

"Hello?"

Silence.

She tried again. "Hello? I'm Elizabeth. We met Saturday at the—er, um—well. I wanted to see if you needed anything. I work across the street at the school and—"

A shuffle sounded from inside, followed by a pan hitting the floor and a swear word.

"—it's okay. No worries. I'll...uh...come back another time. Sorry to bother you."

Before she could head back to the school, the man lurched into the doorway. His jaw obscured by a five o'clock shadow, hair a scraggly mop, he glowered at her intrusion. He held a cast iron pan in one hand, a rag in the other. "I'm not buying it, whatever it is."

"Oh, so you are home. I'm one of the teachers, not a—"

He shook his head. "Not interested."

He reached for the door to pull it shut, but Elizabeth pressed back on the wood. "First impressions last for only seven seconds. I think I messed mine up. What you thought of me. Of everyone. And I'm nice. A teacher. I work here.

Over there," Elizabeth said. She gestured to the school over her shoulder. "You're new in town. I was trying to say I know what that's like, and I wanted to say hello. So you don't feel alone. Like I did."

The man crossed his arms over his chest and appraised her, a silent dressing down.

"I can see it's a bad time. I'll go. I can come back some other time. Have coffee." When the man didn't move, didn't respond, she continued, "Or not."

Elizabeth's cheeks flushed from the effort of digging herself out of the awkward situation. She turned to leave when she heard his voice behind her.

"I'm innocent you know," he said.

"Oh, uh..."

The man shook his head at her, a slow gesture of disbelief. "I've been to prison. That's where I was. Before...Saturday."

Elizabeth gulped and swallowed. "I see."

"I didn't do it, though."

"Uh..."

"It's not your fault, is all I'm trying to say. People weren't going to like me no matter what. So, why bother? Might as well keep my distance."

Elizabeth wrung her hands, aware of her proximity to the house, the distance to the curb of the road. From the playground, the whistle blew. "I should go. That's my cue."

"You don't have to say that to save face," he said. "I don't need your pity. You can go on back over there and tell those biddies all about me. Yes, I'm back, but no, I'm no threat to the kids or anyone else. I'm just trying to live in peace."

"But you're innocent," Elizabeth said.

"What?"

She waved at a pair of her co-workers. The women watched her from the doors, arms folded. Children scampered to line up while the adults leaned their heads together, whispering. "You said you didn't do it, whatever it is, so why would I tell them any of that?"

"Look lady, I've been to prison—"

"Elizabeth."

"Fine. Ms. Elizabeth. You don't have to talk to me. I believe you're a nice person, but don't let my presence force you into any neighborly behavior. Thing is, when I walked through the penitentiary doors, I was as good as guilty. That's a label you can't shake. Now go on back to the kids. Tell 'em not to end up like me."

Elizabeth pressed her lips together and started for the road, her hands in fists. She fought the urge to run away and the urge to turn back. Insist on her goodwill. She paused on the gravel driveway, then faced the former prisoner again.

He stood halfway out the door, like a parent watching a child make the short walk to school in safety.

Elizabeth took a deep breath, then released it. She didn't know what drew her to this man, but this would not be their last conversation.

"Cream and sugar?"

He blinked, struck, as though her words had been an unexpected spitball aimed at his forehead. When recovered, he ran his tongue under his lower lip and squinted his eyes. "Black."

Elizabeth nodded, a short confirmation, and scurried back across the road.

#

As promised, Kade called that night. She'd been watching a Jim Gaffigan special with Casey.

The buzzing of her phone against the coffee table top startled her.

"Good to hear your voice."

"Yeah?"

She wouldn't give Kade any more details about her thoughts until he spilled a few of his own. Elizabeth pictured him in his farmhouse, fresh from the shower. He'd pad around the place in jeans and socks, his hair slicked back and damp. "Busy day?"

"I had some calls to make. Then I needed time to think, sort myself out."

"It's not like you're going to tell me the guy's your father." Kade's revelation that Guy Henderson was his biological contributor, as Kade put it, had been big news. The man's sketchy businesses had almost cost Kade his best mechanic, not to mention Elizabeth's life.

"That he isn't," Kade said. "But he is my uncle."

Elizabeth looked at her phone, then placed it back to her ear. "He what? Am I on a talk show? How many surprise family members do you have?"

Kade was the strong and silent type. He spent more dates asking about her rather than sharing his own history. When she asked, he said other than his mom in Duluth, there wasn't anyone around worth mentioning. Until now.

"You mean, how many more am I hiding?"

"Withdrawn. Sorry, I'm the last person who should judge anyone for not airing family secrets."

Kade sniffed, a sound of resolution. "He's my father's brother and former business partner. Four years ago, he was sentenced to five years for tax evasion."

Elizabeth remembered the man's claim to innocence. "Go on."

Kade sighed and continued. "They launched a tech company together. Cyber-security or something like that. In what will be no surprise to you, not everything was on the books. My uncle went to prison, and my father got to start a new business."

"The drones." That summer, Elizabeth had come up close and personal to Guy's newest money-making scheme.

"Funny how bankruptcy seems to let some people keep most of their money. Anyway, the judge made good on the parole option, and my uncle is out on early release."

Elizabeth traced the family tree of Kade Michaels in her head. "Must have been a surprise to have him back."

"I've got a glass of scotch in hand that agrees with you. Things were...complex with my dad when I was a kid, as you know. My uncle felt sorry for my mom. For me, too. He'd take me to rodeos once in a while. Showed up at my baseball games sometimes. Dropped off presents on my birthday and at Christmas. He was the closest person I had to a father—in a way. When I started to understand what Guy was really doing with those cars, I blamed my uncle, too. Stopped returning his calls. He went to prison, and I didn't visit. When you described the house, and I figured out he was back...it brought up a lot."

"Thanks for letting me know," she said. She started to tell him she'd gone over for a visit that afternoon but held back. She changed the subject instead. "How was the garage today?"

"Not so fast, Liz. Any chance you'd like to talk about your looking for houses?"

8

KADE WAS SILENT WHILE she explained her interests. Jo's encouragement to see what was out there before she made commitments. *Not a lie.* When she finished her explanation, he didn't comment. Instead, he promised to see her later that week.

Elizabeth had his words in mind the next day. Nervous and guilt-ridden, she walked her full thermos across the street. Now, she had two secrets from Kade.

She'd seen his uncle—might as well get used to that title—outside. He'd been elbow deep under the hood of his truck. Elizabeth had lifted her arm in a wave from her spot by the swings. It was a casual greeting, and he nudged his chin her way. She wasn't certain the greeting was an invitation, but it wasn't unfriendly, either.

Besides the thermos, she'd brought a sack of oatmeal chocolate chip cookies. Two had gone in her lunch, two in Casey's, and a half dozen in the bag she'd dropped off with Jo, her ersatz daycare. She'd split the rest between her co-workers and the bag she carried.

On approach to the cabin, she noticed the carport was swept clean of pine needles. A thin ribbon of smoke streaked up from the chimney. Aspens along the opposite side of the creek shook their leaves in the breeze. Like golden coins, they brightened the landscape.

Elizabeth cleared her throat on approach. "I assumed you'd have mugs," she said. "They sell billions of them every year."

He ducked out from under the hood to regard her. When it was evident she wasn't dropping off the treats, he wiped his hands on a rag and headed into the house.

Elizabeth wasn't sure if she should follow or if this was a signal she should leave. She looked at the front door, then to the school, then back to the door. How long should one wait in a state of social uncertainty?

As she stood, indecisive, the door banged open. Kade's uncle returned, pottery wedged under his forearm. He set two mismatched mugs on the truck's bumper and looked at her.

Elizabeth uncapped the thermos and filled the cups with coffee. She withdrew a single cookie from the bag and handed the rest to him. "Pretty spot," she said.

He reached in to withdraw one of the treats, took a bite, and then looked at the cookie while he chewed. When he swallowed, he said, "Maldon sea salt."

Elizabeth nodded. "My grandma's recipe. The chips are something fancy, too, but you'd have to ask my brother Casey why. He sources everything."

"They're good," he said, a gruff admission, and swallowed. "Thank you." He brushed off his hands and took a swig from the mug.

"You never told me your name."

He looked at her, as if considering his response. He shifted his jaw, then replied. "You never asked."

Before Elizabeth could stumble over a reply, he continued.

"It's George," he said. "George Henderson. I thought you knew who I was. What I did. Most people would have cyber-stalked me. Or already have."

Elizabeth crossed her arms. "Why would I have done that?" With the words out of her mouth, she realized her ignorance.

George frowned at her. "You mean you make a habit of visiting felons without first verifying their identity and the crime?"

"Point taken." Elizabeth sipped from her own mug. Next time, she'd bring herself some cream and sugar, somehow. *Next time?* "But we are in full view of the school and all my co-workers."

George looked over the brim of his mug. "Purple Hair is giving me the side eye."

Elizabeth scanned the playground. Maggie lurked at the fenceline. When she saw Elizabeth, she held up her phone and gestured to it. Elizabeth stared at her a moment before she shook her head. Her phone buzzed in her pocket, and she extracted it to read Maggie's message.

"Whatever you do, do not go inside."

"Purple Hair isn't wrong. While I appreciate the coffee, and I can't tell you the last time I had a cookie, it's pretty foolish to show up here."

"I told you I wanted—" Elizabeth stopped. What did she want? A thread of guilt wrapped around each excuse that came to mind. The truth was that she was curious. Curious about this man's story. What he was hiding. She wanted to know about the family Kade never mentioned. If he was dangerous, truly a threat, someone would have told her, right?

"Let me guess—gossip? To kick a guy when he's down. Well, you can save your pity. I don't need it. Never asked for it."

The chirp of the playground whistle sounded from across the grassy expanse. "I guess I was hoping for another concert," Elizabeth said, and risked a wry smile.

When he didn't return her gesture, she reached for the thermos lid, avoiding his gaze. This had been a ridiculous idea. Her co-workers were right. He was right. Her being here was pointless.

George reached for her mug and shrugged. "I learned to play when I was locked up. To pass the time."

Elizabeth looked up. She saw a man weathered by experience.

He sighed. "Bring more of these cookies. Next time."

"You can't keep bringing me food," George said between mouthfuls. "I'll get used to it."

"What person in their right mind argues about a free sandwich?" The last few nights, Elizabeth promised herself she would fess up to George. Tell him about Kade, own her true motivation. It was Friday, which meant she wasn't likely to see George again until Monday. Why was she afraid?

When Elizabeth had requested a second sandwich, Casey hadn't hesitated. A vegetarian, her brother's culinary stacks were loaded with fresh veggies and spread with hummus. She'd been the envy of the lunchroom on more than one occasion. He had to figure she'd be sharing today.

"Not a complaint," he said. "My stove is busted. Guessing mice chewed on some of the electrical. Found someone to look at it next week. Meanwhile it's microwave mac and cheese."

Elizabeth popped a salt and vinegar potato chip in her mouth. George had contributed the bag and two glasses of iced tea for their picnic. They sat at a new picnic table in the yard, the autumn sun sending shadows between the trees.

"I looked you up," she said.

"About time you had some sense."

"So, this place. I mean, I *was* considering buying it and all, but it doesn't exactly scream tech mogul."

George had explained he'd made money creating and selling apps to the highest bidders. "Old family place. Was my father's uncle's fishing cabin. Dad would escape out here. Took the two of us boys sometimes. We loved it. Running wild among the pines, room to roam, and fresh air. He boarded it up in the winter and opened it back up again the next summer. I've always loved this place." George ran his gaze over the modest building and the yard beyond. "They couldn't take it from me because Dad gave it to me in his will. Some kind of legal loophole, according to my lawyer. That's Dad's old truck, too."

Elizabeth risked a question. This was the most she'd heard from George, and her interest bloomed. "But wasn't your brother trying to sell it?"

George snorted. "You mean rob me of what little I have left?" He shook his head. "I gave him power of attorney when I went in. He said he'd protect my assets. I believed him, thought he felt guilty for me taking the hit. Stupid. Instead, he tied up what he could in some new scheme. He was on his way to leeching every last dime from me, and would have, too, if I hadn't come back in the middle of that circus."

"It wasn't the typical open house, that's for sure." Elizabeth rolled up her waxed wrapping. "I am sorry about that."

"Wasn't your fault," George said, taking her trash.

"Glad we got to start over," Elizabeth said.

"Same. Though I still don't get the kindness, I'm not one to look a gift horse in the mouth."

George collected their trash. Elizabeth spotted the edge of a tattoo at his wrist, the end of a vine. Guilt blossomed in her gut. "I've got a confession to make."

"Yeah?"

Words tumbled out of her mouth in a jumble. "I'm dating Kade."

George froze, the sandwich wrappings crinkled in his fist. A muscle in his cheek twitched.

Elizabeth continued. "I didn't know he was your nephew when I met you. When I first met you. But now that you're around and we're starting over and...Kade is so quiet about his life. I thought it would help if I knew...but...I hope we can still be friends..." Elizabeth trailed off.

George withdrew a handkerchief from his pocket and wiped at his mouth. He shoved it back in his pocket and regarded her.

"I'm sorry. I should have said something right after I found out. It wasn't fair. I'll go. I'm sorry."

Elizabeth, shoulders hunched, slunk off the bench. Before she could leave, George called to her.

"Wait. We might be able to help each other."

9

ELIZABETH FOLLOWED HER STUDENTS out the door, backpack slung over one shoulder. The single bus, driven by Maggie—a.k.a. Blue Hair—waited for those who lived farther out. It would wind its way through town and then out along the Wagon Box Road, returning students to their homes.

A group of parents gathered outside the tall chain link fence surrounding the school. Several moms huddled near the small parking lot. One, in oversized sunglasses, held court. She gestured with wide sweeps of her arms, then pointed across the street. The others whispered in hushed, frightened tones. A father leaned against his vehicle and glowered over the group.

Elizabeth drew close enough to overhear their conversation.

"Local or not, he is changing the face of our town."

"He's a convicted felon."

"Right across the street from our kids!"

Elizabeth made a wide arc around the group. She knew the target of their talk. George. Her gut response was to defend him, explain that he'd served time for taxes. Something in her gut kept her quiet. She reached for her car door, eager to get home and put her feet up, only to jump when tapped on the shoulder.

"Jimminy Crickets!"

"Sorry to scare you," Jo said, "but it *is* broad daylight. Clint came home early. He and Rhett are washing Bessie. She got all muddy after that rain. Buck, too, but he won't let us near him with a hose. Probably prefers the stink. Anyway, thought you might hit the trail with me, stretch our legs."

Elizabeth looked over to the small crowd, their volume growing.

"Ignore them," Jo said.

Elizabeth squinted at the group. "You sure? Kids are listening."

"It'll blow over in a week or two. It's boredom and the need to deflect, that's all. Alexis is forgetting the backstory of a boyfriend or two. Nicole's father was at state for most of her teenage years, and Steve is one DUI away from his own consequences. People jump on the chance to get riled up about the misfortunes of others. It distracts them from their own lives."

Elizabeth shifted her attention back to Jo. "All right. Where to?"

At the first turnout for the South Piney Trail, Elizabeth tucked her car off to the side. A small pickup truck and a tan four-door lined the fence. The trailhead was past a narrow opening in a fenceline, wide enough for hikers, horses, and an ATV but not an access road.

Elizabeth fished her sunglasses from her purse before shoving her bag under a seat. She accepted a granola bar from Jo and wedged her water bottle under her arm. Thankful for her choice of footwear that morning, her sneakers would work for the soft earth of the trail. Elizabeth zipped up her hoodie and inhaled the crisp pine air. Jo was right—it was an afternoon for hiking.

Jo shouldered a small pack and set a hat on her head, chin strap loose. She stuffed a small sack in her pocket and her own granola bar into her mouth. "Thought we could keep an eye out for rose hips," she said around the mouthful. "Climbers said they'd spotted some near the cliffs."

"Okay, but why are we really here?" Elizabeth peered at Jo as the women started to walk.

"Can't two friends enjoy an afternoon hike in the woods?" Jo avoided Elizabeth's eyes and scanned the bushes. A chickadee flitted overhead.

"They can," Elizabeth said. She'd picked up her pace to match Jo's long strides. "But I'm a teacher, so I can smell an ulterior motive a mile away. Usually it's someone wanting extra recess or a second helping of pizza. To distract me away from work time. But adults have their agendas too."

"You know me too well," Jo said, and chuckled, a wry acknowledgement. A chipmunk skittered across the soft earth in front of them. Two crows called to each other from among the branches overhead.

Before Elizabeth could press for more, another hiker rounded a bend ahead of them. A silver-haired woman, she could have been the model for an outdoor clothing company. Kitted out in everything from a sun hat to gloves and spotless hiking boots, she frowned at a large, plastic-encased watch on her wrist.

"Hi, Laney," Jo called. "I thought that was your car. How is the trail looking today?"

The woman looked up, a moment of confusion across her face. "Oh, Jo. Hey." With a few steps, she drew nearer, as did they.

Laney peeked around them, over their shoulders, as if to figure out if they were alone. The woman extracted a water bottle from her own pack. Elizabeth spotted an extensive first aid kit tucked into the pack.

"Nice day," Laney said, and took a sip. "Chanterelles are out."

"I heard the same. On our way up to take a peek. See what we can find."

"Got mine," Laney said. She patted her pack as she stowed the water bottle.

"This is my friend, Elizabeth. She teaches at the school."

"Is that so?" Laney removed one glove and extended her hand. "A pleasure."

Elizabeth shook the thin hand, the woman's skin warm to the touch, covered in age spots. "Nice to meet you," Elizabeth said.

"You, too. Always happy to meet a fellow trail fanatic. Careful," Laney said, more to Jo than Elizabeth. "Looks like a little rockslide came down, had to pick my way around."

Up close, Elizabeth saw the deep lines of Laney's face. Heard a waver in her voice. "You know this trail well?"

"Here, other places. I get out as much as I can." Laney glanced past them and down the trail. She slipped her hand back into her glove and adjusted her hat. "Every day God grants me, anyway. Figured if He set me upright in the morning, it's my duty to stay that way until bedtime. I need to hustle. Dinner won't make itself, you know. Bye, girls, enjoy!" Laney hurried off down the trail.

"I like her," Elizabeth said.

Jo had been staring after her friend, eyebrows knitted. "Same. Tough one, that Laney. Older than she looks. Puts the rest of us to shame. Used to work for a big corporation, high level something. I can only guess at the salary she gave up to be here. Got Cushing's, then diabetes, and had to retire early. She and her husband moved out here. Threw out the junk food, became vegans, and the rest—well, you heard her."

"Inspirational," Elizabeth said.

Jo was quiet, as if taking her words apart and reassembling them. "Smart, too. We have new choices every morning. I always think there's a lesson in that."

Elizabeth wondered if Jo meant for herself, Laney, or Elizabeth.

"Big donors to the library," Jo continued. "She and Wallace. Speaking of libraries, do you want to talk about where exactly you want to live?"

"I've got whiplash from that change of subject."

They'd come to a few rocky cliffs, pink and tan, near the rushing water. Jo crouched at a wild rose bush and pinched off one of the hips. The orange-red bulbs were small and bright. "These look good, so now you can earn that granola bar. You heard Laney. Can't stay out here all night."

Elizabeth rolled her eyes and squatted near another bush. "I don't know where I want to live. It's not like I have any money. *But* I want a place. It's like an inner pull. But then there's my brother, and Kade..."

"Catch yourself writing 'Mrs. Elizabeth Michaels' in your notebooks yet?"

Elizabeth laughed. "Not yet, but give me a pink pen, and it might happen."

Jo handed a small bag to Elizabeth. "You wouldn't be the first, nor the last. All joking aside, he's a good man."

Elizabeth scooted over to a new bush. She plucked another rose hip and rolled it between her fingers. "Chock full of vitamin C." She could brew with them, experiment. Maybe a sour ale?

Jo rolled her eyes at Elizabeth's evasion. "Would it kill you to admit you landed a true catch?"

"Kade and I *are* good. Really good. He's great. Especially given...well, everything." Jo knew the couple's history, the complications. "And there's Casey. I went so long without my brother. I love staying at Casey's place. Rhett loves Casey's place."

"But?"

"But...I want Rhett to have a place. Our place. I want him to have security. A stability that I made for him."

"You want a house to prove you're a good mother."

Jo's words hit Elizabeth like a ton of bricks.

It was true. Independence would prove to her son—and herself—that she was a success. She'd have something to which she could point whenever life tried to suggest otherwise. "I hate it when you're right."

Jo regarded Elizabeth for a moment, gave her a sympathetic smile, then said, "I think we've found our share. Shame we didn't see any mushrooms."

"I didn't even know they grew here."

Jo said, "That's not an accident. Good mushroom spots are best kept a secret." Jo stood and stretched, her hands at the base of her spine. "Look, there's nothing wrong with wanting good things out of life. Whether for Rhett or just because. I only want you to see yourself how I see you. How everyone sees you. You already *are* a good mother. A wonderful mom. Rhett doesn't need a house or a pony or anything else to know that. Spend your hard-earned money how you like. As your friend, I don't want you wasting energy on chasing something akin to perfection, that's all. It's a never-ending trail, that one."

They'd started back toward the car. Elizabeth looked out over the view, the winding Piney Creek below them. A breeze passed through the Ponderosa canopy, ticking the needles. She watched the forest, wild and vast, settle itself for the oncoming evening. "Thanks, Jo."

"For what?" A few strands of Jo's hair escaped her hat. Her tan cheeks, a remnant of a summer spent outdoors, were pink from their efforts.

"For holding up a mirror, right when I need to see."

Jo smiled. "Here I thought it was going to be for telling you to tie that shoe before we head back."

Elizabeth checked her sneaker. "That too," she said, and bent down to tie her laces.

"Promise you'll do the same when I need it," Jo said while she waited for Elizabeth. "Straighten me out. And I might need it sooner rather than later. Clint wants us to host Thanksgiving this year—for everyone."

"So, then, no room for us?"

Elizabeth tugged at her laces, pulling them taut. When she did, something shiny glimmered in the dirt. She brushed away the pine needles covering its source.

"The Blaus are definitely invited. No regrets allowed. Danny, too, if he'll come down the mountain. Marj and Randall, too. Heck, the whole neighborhood. I'm going to need all the backup I can get to deal with Clint's sister. She's on one of those new diets. The kind with social media groups and an app. Already sent me a list of what she can't have and we're over two months away."

Elizabeth wasn't listening. Her fingers had uncovered a delicate, gold ring from among the forest debris. It had a small, doubled band and a round, sparkling diamond. She blew the dust off the ring, then held it up to the waning light. "This isn't good," she said. "Does Mother Nature have a Lost and Found?"

Jo stepped closer to peer at Elizabeth's find. "Uh oh. Looks real, too."

"I hate thinking that someone lost it out here." Elizabeth squinted at the inside of the band. "I think there are initials. Oh, this says 14K. But then it says M...something. And...a date?" She wanted to look at it under a lamp with a magnifying glass, take a closer look.

Jo frowned. "Could be anyone's. Trail traffic has slowed with the seasonal shift, but still. You can post a note by the library. I can put something on the hikers' group."

"I'll clean it up with a little baking soda. The engraving has to be a clue."

They were quiet along the walk back. Elizabeth was grateful for the few minutes to consider what Jo said. To take another look at her thoughts.

Elizabeth wasn't yet ready to let go of the dream of a house of her own. She wanted the space, wanted the accomplishment. At the same time, she needed to consider what she'd be giving up. Elizabeth ran her fingers around the ring in her pocket, thinking.

She broke the silence. "Let's say I may need to check my motivation. Reflect a little. How do I figure out what I really want?"

"Don't think there's an easy button there," Jo said. "You could always make a pros and cons list..."

"Is there any situation that can't be solved with a list?" Elizabeth teased. Jo was a die-hard list-making fanatic.

"Nope," said Jo, without hesitation.

Back in the parking lot, Elizabeth's hatchback was one of the two vehicles left.

"Huh," Jo said. "Pretty sure that's Laney's wagon. Thought she'd be long gone."

"A woman that dedicated probably hiked home."

10

ON FRIDAY, MAGGIE AND Rita pulled Elizabeth into the staff lounge.

Maggie held out a chair. "Sit." Rita shot her a look. *"Please,"* Maggie added.

"This is ominous," Elizabeth said. She scooted a chair back and took a seat, her bag on the tabletop.

Rita took the other chair. Maggie dumped an empty donut box into the trash and folded her arms.

"We just want to chat. We're worried about you," Rita said.

Maggie said, "People have been talking."

Elizabeth volleyed her attention between the two women. "Come on, out with it. I've got a kid to pick up."

Rita opened. "We're...concerned. Maybe there's been some confusion. Or unawareness? In complicated situations—"

Maggie interrupted. "Visiting that guy. It's gotta stop. Parents are complaining."

Elizabeth frowned at her co-workers. She'd taken her lunch over to George's picnic table that day. He'd shown her some bird houses he'd made. When she asked about the shop in prison, he'd buttoned up. She changed the subject to asking about his plans for the yard, and the conversation continued. *Must be careful about subjects,* she reminded herself. It was understandable that some things may be off limits.

Elizabeth crossed her arms and slouched into the chair. "I don't understand why anyone cares where I go on my breaks. It's my time. Are parents complaining about me or something?"

"No. About *him.*"

Elizabeth fumed. A flush creeped up her neck and around her ears. "You mean George? He's a neighbor."

Maggie regained the reins. "Liz, he's dangerous. A criminal. Have you stopped to think about what it looks like? You go over there practically every day. You've got a boyfriend."

Elizabeth stood up, the chair shoved backward in her motion. "This has gone too far." She pushed in her chair and slipped the handle of her purse over her shoulder. "I'm leaving."

"Didn't mean to get your blood boiling. I call it like I see it, that's all."

"Enough," Rita said. "You aren't helping." She handed Elizabeth her vest from the rack by the door. "Look, we wanted to ask if you'd thought this through. If you were lonely at work. Maybe we haven't been friendly enough. We know—I know—that you aren't completely happy here. That this isn't your first choice. If we—if I—can be a better friend, will you let me know?"

Elizabeth clutched her purse. It became a defensive shield against this onslaught of accusations. "While I appreciate your inner guilt, you don't need to worry about me. I'm fine. This job is fine. Our working environment is...fine. What is not fine is people butting into my life where it isn't wanted or needed."

Maggie tutted. "Once the handcuffs go on, they never really come off. Keep that in mind."

Elizabeth set her hand on the doorknob, then turned to address her co-workers. "Who I visit when I'm off the clock, whether it's George or anyone else, is my business. Studies show that a separation between work and home is *necessary* for a healthy life. I'm happy to tell anyone exactly where to put any other concerns. *Further,* I would think that people who teach would be the first type to give people second chances. To not judge without all the information. Maybe I'm wrong about that. So if it's okay with my otherwise pleasant co-workers, I'm going to start my weekend now."

She pushed open the door and didn't look back.

11

ELIZABETH GULPED IN THE fresh autumn air. Her footprints crackled on the dried leaves of the sidewalk as she all but ran out of the building.

The contrast between outside and the stuffy break room was palpable. She shivered from head to toe, a realignment of her frustration, and tugged her zipper up to her neck. How could Maggie and Rita have confronted her like that? And at work, too. It was as though they'd planned an intervention. As if she had a bad habit in need of breaking. There was no line on her employment evaluation that prevented her from being nice to others.

Elizabeth stomped the short distance to her car, irked by the opinion that one mistake scarred a reputation for life.

The weekend stretched ahead. Elizabeth said a little prayer of thanks for the expanse of time between the last ten minutes she'd endured and Monday's Pledge of Allegiance. She would need at least that long for her anger to dissipate.

Elizabeth wondered what it would be like to live in a world where every error hung over your head, ablaze in neon lights.

Her drive to the main hub of Story was the equivalent of a couple city blocks. Back out of the school parking lot, head north past the volunteer fire station, take a right at the church. She passed a mother holding hands with two children, an elderly couple, and a man walking the fluffiest golden retriever on a bright orange leash. Would these people also judge her if they knew? Should she embroider the front of her sweatshirt with her mistakes and get it over with?

She made a sharp turn into the post office, the sting of the confrontation still fresh in her mind. She skidded her tires to a quick stop in the gravel. A woman frowned at her entrance, stepping back onto the curb in an exaggerated movement.

"As if I couldn't see you a mile away," Elizabeth muttered from inside the car, then clapped a hand over her mouth. Road rage wasn't her usual reaction. *Come on, Liz, get a grip.*

Elizabeth fished the ring out of her pocket and rubbed at its insides. Cleaned by an old toothbrush and a little baking soda, the diamond sparkled in the afternoon light. She tapped on her phone's flashlight and took another look at the inside of the band. *M.R.H. 8-17-75.*

"Nearly fifty years together is something to be celebrated," she said. "Here's hoping you are still in town."

Outside the post office, the town had erected a sizable chalkboard and smaller cork board. On the cork, pins jabbed everything from business cards to church pamphlets.

The chalkboard was where the day-to-day news took place. Each inch of space was prime real estate for lawn mowing offers, a vacuum for sale, or a lost dog. When one picked up the mail from a post office box, the board was scanned for new information.

In front of the black surface, Elizabeth reached into a shallow dish nailed to one of the support posts. She fished out a nubbin of chalk, disliking the powdery feel on her fingers.

The week had been busy. The board was full of activity including a missing bicycle, a bumper crop of zucchini, and a car wash. In one corner, she wrote her information in careful block letters.

WEDDING BAND FOUND

SOUTH PINEY CREEK

UNIQUE MARKINGS

CALL TO IDENTIFY

Elizabeth figured the note about engravings would deter anyone less than honest. She wouldn't fork over a valuable piece of jewelry on little more detail than, "It's gold, with a diamond in the middle."

Satisfied with her post, she dropped the chalk back in the dish, then stepped back to appraise the placement.

"That's nice of you," came a voice over her shoulder. "Many would have kept it, the owner none the wiser."

Elizabeth found Corbin Beck leaning out of the window of his truck. His hair was wind-tousled. The sleeve of his shirt hitched up to reveal a farmer's tan.

"I didn't think Burro Buddies used a Story postal box," she replied. Elizabeth was unable to resist the man's smile. He'd been a crush for a handful of reasons. The man was a lover of animals, had built a shelter into a thriving rescue business, and he was cute, dang it. Still, when she'd been free, he'd been taken.

The corner of Corbin's mouth turned up. "You'd be right. Saw you at the message board, thought I'd swing by to say hello."

"You know what they say about taking the chalkboard from the teacher." Elizabeth cringed at her own joke the moment it left her lips.

"Glad I caught you. Been meaning to catch up with you and Jo," Corbin added. "I figure we need to start planning the fundraiser."

Elizabeth smacked her hand to her forehead. "I'd completely forgotten."

"No sweat." Corbin put the truck in park and leaned out the window, both arms folded over the sill. "Farm-to-table banquet, silent auction, dog fashion show. We canceled a golf tournament this year because of the weather."

Elizabeth searched her memory for the details, a foothold into their planning. She and Jo had started to talk tablecloth runners and a silent auction. Barn theme. Games for the kids. "Right. Yes. I'm with you now."

"I'm actually wondering about the venue. I know you wanted to have it at the shelter, but with the construction I've got going on, that's not looking good. I'm curious where you and Jo are at with the food and activities? Maybe an update would help me source a new venue. Then I could wrap my head around last-minute prep."

Elizabeth's palms were sweaty, and she wiped them on her opposite sleeves, feigning a chill. She'd completed exactly zero tasks with regard to the event since school started. She didn't know about Jo. "Sure. Yes. I mean, of course. I'd update you now, but I don't want to miss anything from Jo. I'll connect with her and get back to you."

"Great," Corbin said. "Looking forward to it."

Before he could answer, a sheriff's patrol car raced by, lights on.

12

A CLOUD HUNG OVER Elizabeth's mood. On Saturday, she'd scrubbed every surface in the brewery until the place shone like a hall of mirrors.

"You polish that mash tun anymore, and I'll feel guilty using it," Buzz said. He'd been behind the long bar serving the Saturday crowd. He leaned through the doorway between the brewery and the brewing area. "That thing is cleaner than when I bought it now."

"I need to keep busy," Elizabeth said. "If I stop to pause too long, I remember everything that has me irritated." She'd cleaned every inch of the back room, from washing down the floors to dusting the pipes. Anything to keep moving.

"A group of runners took the tables on the side. Mind helping me for a few? I've got them if you could pour some refills."

Elizabeth joined him behind the bar. In sync, they wove around each other, filling orders from different taps.

"Ever regret almost all your life decisions?" Elizabeth squatted in front of the small fridge where they kept non-alcoholic drinks. Buzz, too, kept his favorites in that cooler as he was the only brewery owner Elizabeth knew who did not partake. She selected a can and popped the top before sliding it across the bar to a customer, the probable designated driver for a group of bowling buddies huddled in a booth.

"About every other day at this point," Buzz said. He wiped foam from a glass with a rag before adding it to a tray.

"Aw, Buzz, come on now," Big Ricky said from his stool. "You know you'll miss us when you're beachside, coated in sunscreen. All that sun gets old, you know."

Buzz laughed as he filled another glass at the tap. "I'll send y'all a postcard." To Elizabeth, he said, "How's your plan to strike it rich? This place will be up for sale in a matter of months. That is, if I choose to believe my current contractor."

"Still working on it. I'll let you know if I find any magic lamps."

"You're thinking of selling this place?" Ira slid onto a bar stool next to Ricky. Today he'd worn a button up shirt with the top two buttons undone, with a jacket, half-zipped. Elizabeth could smell his aftershave, saw the pressed lines in his collar.

"Why? You interested in running a brewery?"

"Hey!" Elizabeth tossed a rag at Buzz who caught it, mid-air. "I thought I got first dibs."

"I'm not getting any younger. Might have to entertain any and all offers," Buzz teased her, but there was an edge of truth to his message.

Ira leaned his forearms on the bar top. "I'm more of the silent partner type. An investor. Breweries can be a good place to put your money. Get the right crew to manage a business, and it takes care of itself."

Ira slid his glance to Elizabeth, as though to suggest she might be the right crew. Why was she everyone's second in command in their scenarios?

"Our Elizabeth has her heart set on this place," Ricky added in a show of support. "Killer brewer. And teacher, from what I hear. Just needs a few more pennies. Right, Liz?"

Elizabeth rubbed at her temples. "It's going to take more than pennies, Rick. I need to cut back on all my volunteering, and start charging for all I do."

Buzz frowned, concern creasing his brow. "Did I forget to pay you for the kegs? I swore I gave Casey a check when he brought them."

"Casey is her brother," Ricky whispered to Ira. "He's the catering half of their business."

"No, we're square," Elizabeth said. She shot Ricky a look. "It's Corbin. The big fundraiser. Casey and I offered to cater at cost."

"That was your first mistake," Buzz said. He fit a pint glass under the root beer tap and filled it to the top. He placed it in front of Elizabeth. The cool, creamy beverage was the best he could do while she was serving alcohol to others.

"Tell me about it," she said. Elizabeth sipped at the rim of her glass. The drink had a spicy finish. "We're glad to help, but the guest list keeps climbing. Corbin is thinking he could have two hundred people."

"Corbin was her crush and now boss," Ricky explained, as though the small town translator for Ira. "Well, volunteer boss. Organizer? Anyway—"

"Ricky!" Elizabeth glared at the man, then turned back to Buzz. "It's great for Burro Buddies, but when am I going to have time to prep for that big of an event and work? Gets our name out there, though."

"Got my tickets," Buzz said.

"A fundraiser? Sounds right up my alley." Ira took a big swallow of his lager. "Could you tell this Corbin guy no?"

"No?" Elizabeth turned the answer into a question.

"You know, 'I appreciate you including me, but right now I'm at capacity'—or something like that."

Big Ricky pressed his palms together and affected an English accent. "I've considered your proposal, and given my current goals, I find I cannot assist at this juncture." He and Ira bumped knuckles.

Elizabeth wiped the counter where Ricky's glass had sloshed its contents. She sighed. "If nothing else, it's great exposure to people who would be paying customers. Profit-producing customers. And it's for a good cause."

"It is for a good cause," Buzz said. "Corbin's done incredible work on the place. I've donated for the raffle."

Elizabeth ran both hands down her face before picking up the mop to attack the floor. Buzz carried a tray of beer to the runners, leaving her behind the bar. She tipped up the floor mats to spin figure eights on the tile with the mop.

"Hey, sorry," Ira said. "I didn't mean to step on any toes. I know what it's like to be a small fish in a big pond. Where every challenge is uphill and you never think you'll get anywhere, let alone where you want to be. I worked long and hard with little recognition to get where I am. I know what that haul is like."

"Don't worry about it," Elizabeth said. She watched the mop handle in her hands, let the rhythm soothe her. Maybe it was healthier for her to expect a little less, temper her hopes.

Ira removed his wallet from his back pocket. He extracted a twenty and a business card, then set both on the bar. "I was serious about investing. If you're interested in a potential partnership, call me. Let's talk." With a wave to those seated at the stools, he left them curious.

Elizabeth palmed the cash and card. She walked to the till to make change, then held up the card to read the tiny print on the black background.

"Powder River Basin Ventures," Buzz read over Elizabeth's shoulder. "Sounds legit. Nice guy. Interesting offer. Going to call?"

Elizabeth slid the card into her pocket. "Not likely. I don't want to share my dream with an oversight committee. Running a business with my sibling is all the co-management I need."

"So long as it's on the record that I'm counting down the months—not years—until I throw away my winter gear and live in flip flops. Life is short, Liz. We each have an expiration date."

13

MOTHS FLITTED AGAINST THE great room window. Outside, the yard light cast a yellow circle near the kitchen window. Beneath it, autumnal insects gathered under the beam. Varying sizes and shades of neutral wings hounded the glass.

Elizabeth tracked one of the many creatures. It was Delicate Cycnia. "*Cycnia delicatula*," Elizabeth said aloud.

Casey's headlights traced an arc around the driveway, then disappeared around the side of the house. The disturbance sent a few of those gathered out into the night. She heard a truck door slam and the barn door slide open.

Elizabeth returned to the task in front of her. She'd spread out a yellow pad of lined paper, pencils, a calculator with giant buttons and a stack of bills. On a fresh sheet, she'd arranged numbers in columns, pressed buttons to calculate her worth, and sighed. The results swam in front of her as she tried to cut here, trim there, and inch closer to her goal.

The back door motion light popped on. Stomping boots and a key in the lock signaled her brother's arrival.

"That looks fun," Casey said. He plunked a butternut squash and an onion on the counter.

"As fun as visiting the dentist," Elizabeth said. She doodled a tiny house, complete with trees and a car out front, in one corner of her paper.

Casey glanced over her shoulder. "Flossing ain't going to save you from whatever this is."

Elizabeth furrowed her brow. "I've figured out that if I allow Rhett to develop exactly zero hobbies and start commuting by pixie dust, I'll be able to afford a house...in twenty years." She tossed her pencil on the granite countertop..

"That gives me time to save up for your house-warming present."

Elizabeth buried her head in her hands. "It's hopeless."

Casey flicked the switch on the tea kettle and removed two mugs from the cabinet. At the pantry, he withdrew a couple of tea boxes. "Regular or unleaded?"

Elizabeth lifted her head and spat a lock of hair out of her mouth. "Herbal. I won't need help staying up all night kicking myself. I should have invested at eighteen like all the graduation brochures told me to do."

Casey nodded. "Chamomile, then. Extra honey. And maybe a little whisky."

Elizabeth groaned in response.

"Okay, my cup only."

As Casey busied himself with the mugs, he hummed. Elizabeth frowned at her brother. "What has you in such a good mood? Land a big client? Invent a new cheese flavor?"

Casey lifted a spoon from one of the mugs and set the steaming cup in front of his sister. Elizabeth inhaled, the warmth a balm to her mood. She wrapped both hands around the ceramic surface.

"It's Danny. He received an offer from an investor to go big with his beers."

"Oh?"

Casey took his own mug to the end of the island. "This guy said he moved back into town and is looking for projects. Said Wyoming is a hot market on the heels of Montana. Wants Danny to open a brewery in Buffalo. Apparently, this guy wants to help a string of brewers, says the profit for investors is huge."

Elizabeth sat up. "Reddish, silver hair, dressed like he's from Big Horn? The fancy end."

Casey shrugged. "Don't know. Danny said he seemed legitimate. If the talks go anywhere, I suggested he have Charlie take a look at the deal."

Elizabeth drew her brows together. Was Ira offering a brewery to every brewer he could find? If so, that would mean too many people brewing too much beer. He seemed too focused on profit to do that. The man must be doing his homework, identifying brewers interested—and ready—to take their craft to the next level. "If it's the same guy, he asked me, too. I didn't think much of it."

As she spoke, Elizabeth reconsidered her dismissal of Ira's offer. She looked back down at the dismal numbers that made up her finances. If it was a genuine opportunity, if the terms were decent, she could be on her way to owning her own brewery. Co-owning, she told herself. But still.

"Any interest in mint chocolate ice cream and watching *The Princess Bride* with me? I need to sketch out ideas for new clients."

Exhausted from the calculations and impossible dreams, Elizabeth said, "I'll get the bowls."

14

"ROSES?" SHE BENT HER head to sniff the fragrant blossoms.

"And they're pink," Casey said from the couch. He'd slouched in front of a football game on the big screen, remote in hand. "Subtle, yet indicative. Don't let him ruin your reputation tonight, sis."

Kade swept off his hat and bowed. "I have nothing but honorable intentions toward your sister."

Casey lifted one eyebrow. "Every cowboy says that about my sister."

Kade grinned, his five o'clock shadow not enough to mask the dimple Elizabeth loved. "That's a streak I hope to break."

Jo called out from the kitchen. "Is that Kade?" She held a big silver bowl in her arms. With a whisk, she whipped at the contents. "Would you ask him to close up the barn before he takes off his boots?"

"Yes, Mrs. Wolf," Kade said. "Benny, you want to come with?"

"No, thank you." Benny had unpacked a selection of rock finds and placed them in front of Rhett. He arranged them in careful rows and began to explain their merits. Heads together, the two boys examined the rock collection.

"I'll go," Elizabeth said, handing her bouquet to Casey.

"You kids have fun," her brother teased, and returned to the game.

Elizabeth slipped into her shoes and followed Kade out the front door. They crossed the yard toward the barn as though on a casual stroll.

Inside the building, Bessie and Buck waited in their stalls, chewing the last of their dinners. The adopted donkey and her goat buddy regarded Elizabeth and Kade with interest. The goat climbed to the highest platform in his stall, still chewing, as though to assert casual dominance.

Kade checked each door, giving them a quick rattle to verify integrity. Elizabeth peered into the water trough, then slipped each animal a ginger snap from her pocket. Closing down a barn was part routine, part chance to give your four-footed, winged, and other animal friends a snug goodnight.

"Lights out," Kade said, and flipped the interior switch.

Elizabeth closed the pair of doors and slid the bolt through the latch. When she turned around, Kade was close. So close.

"Hey," he said.

"Hey."

Stars scattered across the inky sky above Kade's head, but all Elizabeth saw was the light in his eyes. In that moment, she was light, airy. It was as though she could give over all her concerns to him.

She shook her head, the slightest movement. This was when it was challenging to cling to goals. When another person could make something so easy. But it wouldn't be the same. Couldn't be.

Kade leaned in and tilted his face. He was centimeters from her lips when she spoke. "Most of our night vision ability is accessible after the first five minutes in the dark."

"Is it?" he whispered into her ear.

A shiver snaked down Elizabeth's spine. Before she could reply, a car swung into the driveway from the road. Reflective paint flashed silver in the dim. A sheriff's patrol car, off duty.

Elizabeth and Kade sprang apart. Kade rubbed at the back of his head, sheepish. "Why do I feel like I was caught doing something naughty?"

Elizabeth reached for his hand with one of hers. "What were you up to in high school?"

"I watched a few movies, that's all," Kade said. He held tight to her hand as they walked back to the house. "I was never brave enough to go after the girl."

Elizabeth gave his hand a squeeze. "What changed?"

Kade stopped and faced her. The grin had dropped from his face, replaced by a steady gaze. "Life got short. Priorities shifted. I got real clear on what I want." He brushed his lips across Elizabeth's, a soft gesture that spoke volumes.

When they stepped into the light of the occupied kitchen, silence was the first sign something was wrong. The second was the look on everyone's faces.

Sheriff Wolf stood in the center of the room in full uniform, hat and all. Casey and his overfilled wine glass occupied a seat at the small, round table. He stared into the liquid. Elizabeth's roses lay abandoned on the tabletop, a water-filled vase next to them.

"What happened?" Elizabeth listened for the boys in the living room. Benny chattered away at Rhett. "What's going on?"

Jo, in her vintage, ruffle-edged apron spattered with marinara, set them in motion. "I'll get you both a glass."

Kade pressed, residual cheer in his voice. "All right, who died?"

"Laney Horowitz," Clint said. He reached out a hand and placed it on Kade's shoulder.

"I'm so sorry, Kade," Jo said. She set a glass in front of him and squeezed his shoulder. "We're here for you, whatever you need."

Kade looked down at the glass, then out the darkened kitchen window. Without another word, he walked back out the kitchen door and into the night.

15

THE SCENT OF HAY filled Elizabeth's nostrils for the second time that evening.

"Thought I'd find you in here," she said into the dim.

Jo had insisted she wait a few minutes in the quiet kitchen. No one said much as Jo stirred a pot and peeked into the oven. When she proclaimed dinner would be ready in fifteen minutes, Elizabeth took the opportunity to head outside with the message.

Now, inside the big building, a chill seeped in through the cracks in the walls. Bessie stomped a hoof, a muted thump against the floor beneath them. There was a sniffle, then a brusque, "Did Jo send you out?"

"With a message that dinner is almost ready. Smells good, too." Elizabeth stepped outside the ring of the yard light and into the gloom. The oversized bulb suspended over the back porch gave little help in the barn. As she moved farther from the door, darkness snuck in around her. She could make out the shape of Kade, a phantom-like figure stroking Bessie's flank.

He wiped at his eyes with one hand, an almost imperceptible movement. "Thanks for giving me a few minutes to myself."

Elizabeth bit her bottom lip. She was torn. Her insides pushed her to reach for him. Provide comfort for his grief. Laney, the woman from the trail, alive and active one day, was gone the next. There was a mystery here, with Kade. Her gut propelled her to the edge of the stall. She leaned her arms on the small gate and waited.

Kade pushed back from the stall and sighed. In response, Buck thumped against his stall, a warning. "Easy, Buck. It's still me." To Elizabeth, Kade said, "Goat eyes are kind of freaky in the darkness."

"They're kind of freaky all the time," Elizabeth said. "It gives the genus *Capra* a wilder field of vision, though. Everything helps when you're prey."

Kade snorted. Elizabeth was thankful her endless stream of facts provided a moment of levity. A habit since childhood, it was a habit of nerves she'd yet to shake.

"I can guess what you're wondering. Laney is...was...like a surrogate parent for me."

Elizabeth thought back to the older woman she'd met on the trail. Hiker shirt, hair a practical length, curled out of her face. Sunglasses affixed to her head with a colorful strap, first aid kit. She hadn't known there'd been any connection before.

"Laney taught me to be...decent. Even when it's hard. Or when you have to hide that decency from others. When you know people are wrong and are treating others like garbage. She was the opposite of that. She gave a damn and risked her own neck to show it."

Elizabeth watched Kade's shadow shift positions. He stared forward, as though watching a movie of Laney's good deeds play against the barn wall.

"She sounds like a person with some serious integrity. I wish I could have known her better. We need more people like that."

"Yeah, we do."

Kade exhaled, a slow release of pressure. She heard the kitchen door open and guessed Jo was assessing their progress. "I'd love to hear more about her. If you want to tell me, that is."

Elizabeth's eyes had grown accustomed to the dark. In the barn, Kade was still, focused. The sharp lines of his face stood out in the shadows. He pressed his lips together and then gave a slight nod.

"Forgive me for not saying anything before. I was told for so long never to mention her name."

16

K ADE SHIFTED UNTIL HE was next to Elizabeth, as though keeping his voice low eased the telling of an old secret. "Laney made my mom promise not to say anything. Then when I was old enough to notice what was going on, she made me promise, too."

"Secrets are hard on kids," Elizabeth said. Her comment came from experience.

"They were. I guess the truth can't hurt anyone now, can it? I know I told you before what kind of man Guy was to my mom."

"I remember." That summer, she'd learned Guy left his pregnant girlfriend the moment he'd heard the news. He denied his son's very existence until one day he wanted a son, and it was too late.

"Laney worked for him. She was his secretary. Administrative assistant, as they say now. Worked for him for over twenty years, retired when I graduated high school."

"That's quite the relationship."

Elizabeth had brushed up against one of Guy's other employees that summer. She'd ended up in the trunk of a car, and Guy slipped out from under any consequences.

Kade kept the man at arm's length. He'd gone this long without a terrible father around, and he saw no need to change. "The way my mom told it, the minute Laney found out about me, she stormed into his office and demanded he do something. He refused, of course. Threatened that if she meddled in his personal life again, she could look for another job—and over her shoulder."

"That's quite the ultimatum. "

"So, she kept her mouth shut. To him. Mom said one day Laney showed up at her job, slipped her an envelope stuffed with cash, and begged her not to say a word. Promised she'd deliver more when she could."

"What did your mom do?"

"Kept her mouth shut, that's what." Faint hooting alerted a great horned owl was near, and Kade turned his head toward the noise. When the sound faded, he continued. "For years."

Elizabeth flexed her wrists. She'd gripped the edge of the stall until her knuckles whitened. "Takes guts to do that. Both of them."

Kade reached for Elizabeth's hand in the dark. "Laney brought me birthday presents. Christmas presents. I'd so much as mention to mom that I wanted a new truck, or a baseball bat, and it would be under the tree. Now, I know my mom and Laney talked, but when I was little, it seemed like Santa came, got my letters and everything. Like he actually cared about this random kid from the sticks."

"How did you find out it was her?"

"There was this one time when Laney picked me up from school. Mom had a flat, and I'd had baseball practice. The other guys had all left, and Mom must have called her, desperate. Here she came, Dad's secretary. Took me to get ice cream. She asked me all these questions...I think she was trying to figure out if I'd turned out like him."

Elizabeth couldn't decide on the best response, so she stayed quiet, thinking.

Kade continued, "I graduated. Went to school in Laramie. It wasn't until I saw who footed the bill for school that I asked questions. Mom was tight-lipped, telling me that if Guy knew, he'd find a way to punish Laney, even now."

"We can't hold onto that kind of blame and expect to move forward."

"The older I get, the better I understand that," Kade said.

They moved toward the door and into the moonlight. The night air was still, filtered. A soft flap of wings indicated the owl's departure.

Elizabeth could see Kade's face, clearer in the moonlight. This moment could be the bridge she'd been looking for. The opportunity to tell Kade she'd met George. Chatted with him, was half considering him an acquaintance of sorts. "Speaking of the past..."

"Any chance we can save it for after dinner?"

After dinner, Casey whisked Rhett home to bed and Kade left with a sleepy Benny. Elizabeth joined Clint and Jo in the kitchen.

Leia sprawled on the tile. The bright lights had no effect on her ability to sack out. Elizabeth's four-legged best friend emitted a soft snore, her front paw twitching in her sleep.

"They found her by the creek."

Jo had been scrubbing a pot. She paused, her hand in the sudsy water. "She drowned?"

Clint rattled off the details he knew. "Cardiac arrest. They think. Autopsy will get us closer to certainty."

"Worst kind of news," Jo said. She returned to scrubbing. "How'd Wallace take it?"

"How would I take it?"

A look passed between the Wolfs. Elizabeth recognized love and fear in their eyes. Heart-rending attachment to each other. Despair at knowing one day, one of them would have to say goodbye first.

Clint wrapped his arms around his wife and gave her a tight hug. Jo's arms, dish rag in one, pot in the other, fell to her side as she leaned into him and closed her eyes. Elizabeth wondered if she should leave the two to their comforts, but then Clint released his wife and shrugged back into his coat.

"Think I'll take the pack for a walk, assuming that's okay with both of you?"

Elizabeth and Jo nodded. From the living room, Clint gave a short whistle, and the grunt and scuffle of dogs followed. Leia roused herself from the kitchen floor and padded off to follow them.

"He's worried about me," Jo said. "Has been since last summer, when...well, you know."

Elizabeth knew the story of Jo finding a deceased woman on a trail, her stumble over the killer's identity, and the danger she'd been in last summer.

"He's one of the best," Elizabeth said. "May the rest of us girls end up so lucky."

"All right, spill."

Jo listened, suds again filling the basin, as Elizabeth debriefed her conversation.

"I get it. Benny has been the light of his life since he was born. He wants to put the world on a platter for him, and I understand that."

Benny had come to live with his uncle Kade when his mom went to prison. Benny's father was absent more than he'd ever been present.

"Kade knows what it's like to be abandoned," Jo said. She finished loading the rack and tipped the dishwasher door closed. "A man doesn't unburden himself to you like that with no end. He *wants* you to get things about him."

"Why does it feel like every time I start to feel like I understand him, something flares up, and I feel like I know nothing?"

Jo wiped her hands on a dishtowel. She opened the plastic container holding the rest of the brownies and held it out to Elizabeth. "Be glad you have someone to worry over. Laney's husband no longer has that luxury."

17

ON THE WAY INTO work, a bluster of leaves whisked past Elizabeth. They whipped up in a gust before colliding with the side of the brick school building. Red, yellow, brown, and orange collected in the alcove, a testament to the changing of seasons. Elizabeth was thankful for the evergreens that held their color when winter blanketed the world in white. But there was a certain magic in the transition of deciduous leaves. A sunset, temporary and volatile.

Elizabeth tucked the end of her scarf back under one of the loops. Uniform, puffy clouds darted across the sky. Chimney smoke scented the mountain air.

Elizabeth had the urge to decorate with pumpkins and sunflowers, copper and hazelnut. A centerpiece on the coffee table, a garland on the mantle. She could hunt for decorations in town.

It was tough having a designer for a brother. He wanted clean lines and tame neutrals while Elizabeth wanted to bring the outside in. She could sweeten a request with some mulled wine and a pot of curry. A stop at the small market in Story on the way home. Sauté the aromatics, add veggies, and in under an hour, she'd be on her way to autumn at the Blau House.

For her colleagues, she'd decided to take a step toward peace. That morning, she'd brewed a pot of coffee and plunked down a plate of apple cider donuts. Casey had been experimenting on bite-size desserts for their catering business. That weekend, he'd churned out tray after tray of goat cheese-based treats. The results, cinnamon-dusted and smelling of heaven, were a welcome offering.

"I'm going to need that recipe," Rita told her. "Actually, don't tell me. I shouldn't own that kind of weapon. Just promise me you'll make them for my birthday. And Christmas. Tuesdays, too." Rita tucked a second golden circle in her lunchbox.

Maggie had filled her thermos with coffee, balanced a donut on top, and nodded at Elizabeth.

They were on steady ground, once again. For now.

That morning, Elizabeth had packed a second sack of the pastries. She debated dropping it off before work, but Kade's truck was in George's driveway.

Elizabeth ducked inside the school to avoid being seen. From the window of the small cafeteria, she watched Kade lower the truck bed. Gloves on, he unloaded lumber from the bed. George joined him, the two making quick work of the load. Elizabeth shelved her plan.

Now, with the students at lunch recess, Elizabeth checked the progress across the street. The men had framed out a small shed-like structure near the creek. A skeleton of boards held its shape, the pitch of its roof ready for snow.

The pair came out of the house to stand by Kade's truck, talking. At one point, George held out his hand. Kade shook it before getting into his truck. The moment he pulled out of the driveway, the school yard would be in Kade's full view. Including his girlfriend, staring in his direction.

Elizabeth eyed the chain link fence behind the backstop. Nowhere to hide. The playground structure, swings, teeter-totter, and slides were across the yard. Guilt spurred panic.

"Get a grip," she said. "It's your boyfriend." The third grader who'd just caught a kickball gave her a look. "Good catch, I mean."

When she looked back, Kade had already crossed the road to the school's small parking lot. His truck idle, he rolled down the window. "Thought I recognized that scarf."

"Oh, hey," Elizabeth returned. "I saw your truck."

"Any chance I could sneak a kiss from my girl?"

"Not with the kids watching. I'd never live it down."

The corner of Kade's mouth turned up. "Rain check, then. Dinner. Saturday night—bring Rhett?"

"I'll check with Rhett's secretary, but I think he's free."

"Then pencil me in?"

This was her guy. They were a team. She wanted to kiss him. But the sound of the kids behind her and her lingering guilt held her back. "How about I bring dessert?"

"Deal. Oh, and Liz?" He met her gaze from across the pavement. His eyes were a darkening amber, her favorite autumnal shade. "Thanks for the other night. Got me thinking. Really thinking. I've got a surprise for Saturday night."

With a wave, he drove off in a swirl of fallen leaves.

Hushed voices sifted out from the front room of the Women's Club, a tidy building next to the library in Story. Elizabeth entered from the back. Trays of mini chicken salad sandwiches, stuffed mushrooms, and brownies rested in a box in her arms.

"Good, you made it," Jo said, wringing her hands together. She surveyed the cramped back room and whisked a stack of files and a box of Christmas decorations off a table. "Go ahead and put them on there. I'll shove these in the closet, and then we can get things set out."

Jo fished a list from the pocket of her navy wrap-around dress. She'd pinned up her hair, and a simple set of pearls adorned her earlobes.

"The flowers are here. You're here with the food. The pastor should be here any minute. I like your dress by the way." Jo had paused her list long enough to take in Elizabeth's outfit.

"Thanks." Elizabeth had tugged on the single dark dress she owned only to realize the last time she'd worn it was to Justin's funeral the year before. *I've got to go shopping,* she thought. "Should I set food out?"

"Not yet. Tasha is still setting up the coffee bar area. She gets territorial if you don't let her finish. I'll give her five more minutes and then cut her off from napkin folding. We got a couple of the orchestra students to play—Shelly volunteered her kid who brought a friend. The only thing we need now is for everyone to take their seats, and we can get started."

"I'll unwrap the trays in here. You tell me when it's safe to bring them out."

"Great idea. I'll go see if I can light a fire under Tasha."

In the hallway, the walls were lined, floor-to-ceiling, with photo collages. Hundreds of photos filled the space, the decades marching by.

From the photographs, Elizabeth guessed the club had been around for a few generations of Sheridan County women. There were dresses with drop waists, combs and barrettes pinning back finger curls. Farther down, clothing shifted, variety eking its way into the fashion. A rainbow of synthetic fabrics and the occasional pair of jeans, followed by pastels and shoulder pads. Recent photographs had women wearing everything from gardening gear to sequined tops. The wall of friendship made Elizabeth smile.

They'd built and sustained a community. That very community is what brought them together that night. What would it be like to be a member, to have her own picture end up on that wall?

In the main room, mourners filled every inch of the space with their bodies and their voices. Bouquets occupied every surface. A stream of people entered, greeted each other, and sought a space to sit.

Jo bustled over to where Elizabeth waited. "Okay, let's grab those trays as I need people to load up their napkins and sit. We've only got a few minutes before we're due to start."

Together, Elizabeth and Jo set out the offering, and people took turns loading up napkins. The somber mood was punctuated by the occasional exclamation.

"I've got to start making these. So creamy."

"Can you ever get enough chocolate?"

"Let me snag a second one, and then we should take a seat."

With mouths full, the room quieted as attendees shifted toward the rows of folding chairs. Elizabeth did a quick count—forty, with a few standing.

Elizabeth hovered near the food table, in case refills were needed. In front of her, a massive ring of flowers framed a memorial sign. When a latecomer bumped the arrangement,

Elizabeth scrambled to catch the display. As she steadied it back onto the stand, she read the large, elegant script.

Celebrating the life of
Melanie Rae Horowitz
Beloved wife, mother, and grandmother
Loved beyond words and missed beyond measure.

Jo stepped behind a small podium placed near the hallway, the only space left in the room. She cleared her throat as stragglers took the last seats or stood on the edges of the room.

"Thank you all for coming. I'm not one for big speeches, as you know, but Laney was a treasure to this community. There isn't a person in this room who wasn't inspired by her list of good deeds, me included. Her absence is a tragedy. My and the sheriff's heartfelt sympathy to her family. May she rest in peace." Several heads nodded and a few uttered a soft *Amen*. Jo continued, "Now, her husband, Wallace, would like to say a few words."

An elderly man stood to shuffle up the aisle. He wore dark slacks and a buttoned cardigan over a tie dotted with sailboats. He was trim, like his wife, with freckles covering his bald scalp and a Santa Claus beard. This man was the cheerful next-door neighbor type. The one who would show you how to use a power tool, bounce his grandkids on his lap, and build model trains in his garage. At the microphone, tears leaked from his eyes as he summoned the courage to speak. A woman in the front row pressed tissues into his hand. He licked his lips and consulted a piece of paper he held.

"Laney hiked every day. Said it was how she worked through her problems, came up with ideas, and gave praise to this gorgeous landscape. To stay young, she'd tell me. For if God ever found her idle, what reason could he have to keep her here? She didn't want to miss a moment of life, you see. Every challenge that came that woman's way was only a stepping stone. Something she'd look back on in triumph. I loved her like a rose loves the sun, the giver of light. She made me a better person, gave me life."

Here, Wallace squeezed his eyes shut, then brushed away tears with a wrinkled hand. He sniffed, and Jo reached over to give him a hug. She whispered in his ear, and he nodded, gathering himself. Once again, Wallace returned to the microphone.

"Thank you for loving my beautiful wife. There's no way I could have told her enough, shown her enough how much she meant to me. I don't know how to say goodbye to forty-eight years with an angel. Now that she's gone..." Wallace choked up, then took a breath to steel himself. He began again. "Now that she's gone, I hope you'll help me keep her memory alive."

There were few dry eyes left in the room when Wallace returned to his seat. Those around him patted his arm, offered sympathy. Elizabeth brushed her own tears from her cheeks. Wallace's words had broken nearly every heart in the room.

The pastor spoke next, highlighting Laney's dedication to the community and the challenges grief provides. A few of those gathered chose to share their own stories about Laney, then the pastor said a closing prayer. Creaky knees and quiet mourning took over as guests began to leave their seats.

This was Elizabeth's cue to set out the mini chocolate chip cookies and pumpkin donut holes. Jo refilled the coffee urn with a carafe. She'd known many would linger, unwilling to sever ties with the night until they'd spoken with everyone.

Elizabeth watched attendees console each other, share hugs and words of kindness. Wallace hovered near the door, accepting the comfort that flowed his way. She watched him sink into every hug, each offered shoulder. What would it be like to be married for nearly five decades? To have someone cherish her as Wallace did Laney.

Jo approached her side. She followed Elizabeth's gaze and said, "May we all be so lucky."

Elizabeth nodded. "You're practically there."

"Feels like it, some days," Jo said. "I'll have to tell Clint to get started on my eulogy. He'll need a few decades at least to get half as heartfelt as Wallace. That man loved his wife something fierce."

"There are good things about a good marriage," Elizabeth said. Jo opened her mouth to reply, but Elizabeth shook her head and continued. "I know that, deep down. But I'd forgotten, you know? Nick and I weren't like that," she said, gesturing to Wallace. "We were never like that. I'd love to feel that way about someone. Have them feel that way about me."

"May we all be so blessed," Jo said.

18

ELIZABETH TOOK THE LONG way into town. Her car skipped a few exits until she'd need to drive past Kade's Garage. She was ahead of schedule, and he'd been scarce that week. If pressed, she would have admitted his promise of a surprise had kept her up all week.

After the memorial service, Elizabeth remained thoughtful. A new layer of sadness crept in. It was the kind that arrives when you've seen into the future and known that this life is fleeting. Remembered that your place, this time, has an end date. With her own mortality in mind, Elizabeth considered her choices.

Wallace's words had sunk deep within her, found a need she'd buried. Still, independence tugged at her subconscious. It was as though the two ideals waged a civilized war in her heart. She wasn't sure which she wanted to win.

Today, despite a pressing to-do list, she couldn't tear her mind from Kade. What if he asked her to move in with him? After the service, had she changed her mind?

Kade's truck wasn't in the lot. Part of Elizabeth sagged in relief. Her emotions were a jumble, like fireflies in a jar.

In front of the shop, Alma's Tardis was on full display. The amateur mechanic's classic Mustang sparkled from a recent wax. Off the clock, Kade's employees worked on their own cars. Over the summer, Alma made incredible progress on her restoration.

"I can see myself in the chrome," Elizabeth called in greeting. "Guessing the engine is also spotless."

Alma left the bays to meet Elizabeth at the car. She lifted her face shield up and over her head. "Hey there. Not quite spick and span, but she's getting there."

"What's next?"

"Upholstery. Sky blue leather. I don't trust myself to do that, yet. I've got to send her either up to Billings or down to Casper. Kade's going to put in a few calls for me, see what he can do."

Alma took the job at Kade's when a lack of funds kept her from finishing an arts degree. A budding documentary maker, she swore she'd get back to films one day. Meanwhile, she picked up a steady—and lucrative—set of skills.

"Speaking of your boss—he out for the day?"

Alma lifted her shoulders in a brief shrug. "Your guess is as good as mine. We've slowed down a bit. Nothing Raj and I can't handle. Said he'd take a day off, something he never does. Should I tell him you stopped by if he shows up?"

"I'll call him," Elizabeth said, not sure if she would. She wondered if his project was more work at George's house. She ran a finger along the top of one of the side mirrors. "Keep at it, Alma. She's a beauty."

The bell over the door at Beans & Biscuits jangled. The familiar sound was a comfort akin to the scent of muffins, cookies, and crusty bread inside the cafe. Jo and Corbin had claimed a booth, heads together.

Elizabeth made a stop at the front counter.

"Usual?" Gary Price shifted a dozen danishes, warm from the pan, to their spot on a shelf. A circle of steam formed on the glass.

"Indeed. And save the last one of that batch for me. Those smell like heaven." Elizabeth detected hints of nutmeg, cloves, and a healthy dose of ginger.

"Enid's newest creation." Gary held up the swirls of pastry, a delicate center of jam, with a pair of tongs. "Want a plate—or should I set up an IV so you can mainline the sugar?"

"You may need to roll me out of here after I inhale the thing. How does Enid get them so perfect?"

"Pure stubbornness," Gary said as he slid the danish onto a plate and set it in front of Elizabeth. Gary adored his boss. "They dare not disappoint the artist."

"May she always find her muse."

Gary reached for a mug and prepared to make Elizabeth's favorite, a dirty chai. One part spiced black tea, one part steamed milk, and a shot of espresso. "This will be out in two minutes. Meanwhile, you'd better get over there. Those two will sign your free time away if you don't wrangle in their plans."

Elizabeth took her plate to the table and slid in next to Jo. "So, what did I miss? Gary made it sound like y'all are engaging in an epic battle of Risk over here."

"Don't tempt me with that thing," Jo said, pushing at Elizabeth's plate. "Clint and I have kicked sugar for the week. I'm going to climb the walls. Do you know how dull this cappuccino is without any of the good stuff? It's like I went to Italy and closed my eyes in the museums."

"I wouldn't share if you begged me," Liz said. "This tasty morsel and I have a date with destiny."

"Better get one for myself," Corbin said. He scooted out of the booth. "Especially if we are about to do battle over a barn dance."

When he was out of earshot, Elizabeth raised an eyebrow. "Barn dance?"

Jo lifted one shoulder. "Might have been my idea. C'mon, it's cute. Think of the costumes."

"I thought you hate costumes." Elizabeth remembered their night at the murder mystery party.

"I looked ridiculous as a Roman god. But I have a perfect paisley skirt and a brand new pair of boots. When else will I get Clint to dance?"

"You, fine. Me and dance are not two words you'll find in the same sentence."

"Good," Jo said. "Because you'll be too busy running things to have any fun. That's for the guests."

"Sounds a lot like my wedding," Elizabeth said, and took a bite. She moaned as she chewed.

"Now you're being cruel," Jo whined.

Corbin returned with his own treat and Elizabeth's beverage. "Gary said if they ever do commercials, you're hired."

Elizabeth shot Gary a thumbs up. "I'm in. As long as more of these are in my future."

"Stop," Jo said. "This is torture. Can we please focus on the event?"

Corbin grinned at Elizabeth and pushed his plate off to the side. He took a small notebook from his jacket pocket and opened it to a page of notes. A strand of hay stuck out of his hair. Elizabeth restrained herself from plucking it off.

"All right. What are my marching orders?"

"Our goal is to raise enough to put in another set of kennels."

Burro Buddies had expanded into a new facility with a donation from a widow, Hannah Black. He'd gone from an unknown animal rescue agency of one to the owner of a premiere shelter. He rehabilitated retired sports dogs into companions and therapy animals. Now, he advised, lobbied, and otherwise continued to fight for animals.

Elizabeth and Jo had helped him launch the training component. They'd volunteered countless hours and had more coming.

Corbin scratched some numbers on his notepad. "With ticket sales, the auction, and maybe a raffle or two, I think we can get there."

"I'm in," Elizabeth said.

Corbin clapped his hands together. "Love it."

"Good," Jo said. "Because it's only a couple of weeks away. Oh, and we still need items for the auction, the menu, and a venue. And the music, too."

Elizabeth gulped. "We don't even have a venue?"

"Have time for a field trip? I was thinking we could host at Burro Buddies," Corbin said. "Why don't you both come check it out? Bring Rhett. I've got some new fur babies.

"Kittens?"

Corbin nodded. "Found them in a shopping cart. Darlings, as always. Tuxedo mix."

Elizabeth sighed. "Rhett will be smitten, as usual. This afternoon?"

19

ELIZABETH SWALLOWED HER PRIDE along the drive.

Last winter when she'd found Leia, Elizabeth had grown attached to Corbin's former location—and a little to Corbin himself. He'd built a hodgepodge of buildings, each styled like a building in an old western town. Elizabeth had loved her visits.

Until Hannah Black.

Hannah was the widow of a famous sled dog breeder and trainer. When Hannah returned to town for the funeral of her estranged husband, it hadn't taken her long to rekindle an old flame—Corbin—and clash with Elizabeth.

Elizabeth couldn't blame Hannah, not for long, anyway. Corbin was the other half of that equation. Even if his flirtation with Elizabeth had been real at first, feelings change. The past was a powerful pull, and Hannah didn't force Elizabeth's wounded pride. Life moved on, and so would she.

Still, her arrival at the new facility stung a little. Hannah had donated land for the building, a convenient spot next to her own spread. Corbin built a huge barn and would soon add kennels. He opened his doors for as many animals as he could manage and had started hiring staff.

There was no sign of anyone when Elizabeth arrived. She extracted Rhett from his car seat and made her way to the corrals. Rhett loved the new small herd of Sicilian donkeys. Corbin took them in from a New Mexico facility that was out of space. Elizabeth's son loved to pat the tops of their heads to watch their ears drop in reflex.

In a snug stall at the back of the corrals, a single donkey was tethered by a lead rope. A person in coveralls hunched over one of the animal's hooves.

"Hello there," she said. "I'm here to meet with Corbin. Seen him around?"

Elizabeth's eyes widened when the person unfolded from their bent position.

George wiped at his forehead with the side of one arm. "This is unexpected." He looked from Elizabeth to Rhett and back. "Corbin said something about the ducks."

"I didn't know you...work here." Rhett toddled around the corral bars toward George. The man watched him, blinking.

"He was hiring. Gave me a shot."

Elizabeth looked from George to the tools. "I didn't know farrier school was part of a computer science degree."

George snorted. "Not quite, I picked this up elsewhere. There was a wild horse inmate program. I did well, so I qualified for the certificate."

"And spent time with wild horses?"

"Tame, too. Helped pass the time. And it got me some gainful employment. Takes care of my parole requirements. Corbin is going to train me to work with the dogs next. Take them out to meet people. Said if I bond with a dog, I can take 'em home. Be the face of his business."

Elizabeth frowned. She thought of herself as the ambassador for the sled dogs. Well, her and Leia. She tasted a bitterness to her saliva, and goosebumps crawled up her arms. First, he took Kade's attention, and now Corbin's. Was she jealous—of a convict? Maybe Maggie and Rita were right. Her friendship with George had consequences she was only just starting to learn. "Do you think that's a good idea?"

George narrowed his eyes. "What exactly are you asking?"

Elizabeth's cheeks flushed. She'd crossed a line, put her petty insecurity on display. Before she could back pedal, change the subject back to Rhett, Corbin came out of his office.

"Elizabeth, George, I see you've met. Rhett, my man. Want to come see the kittens?"

Corbin took the little boy's hand and led him inside. Elizabeth hurried to follow, but she couldn't escape the stare boring holes in her back.

20

ELIZABETH HUSTLED RHETT THROUGH Kade's front door, her triple chocolate cheesecake in a tote over one arm. Inside the hall, she peeled the wet rain coat off Rhett and removed his yellow rain boots. The little boy headed down the familiar hallway to find his playmate, Benny.

Her own coat dripping, Elizabeth kicked out of her muddy boots and fluffed her hair. With a glance in the hall mirror, she headed for the kitchen.

At the doorway, her feet refused to walk any farther.

On one side of the island, watching Kade stir a sauce pot with a wooden spoon, was George.

Oh boy.

"Great," Kade said, his face alight. "You're here." He gave her a quick kiss on the cheek, then stood back and clasped his hands.

"Hello," Elizabeth said to George, lobbing the ball in his court.

"Hello."

A volley, she thought. *Now what?*

"Elizabeth, this is my uncle." Kade gestured between the two of them. "And, George, this is the woman I was telling you about."

"More like gushing about," George said. He stood with his hand extended.

Elizabeth shook his hand, and his eyes said, *I won't tell if you won't.*

Crud. No immediate acknowledgement equaled pretending she and George didn't know each other. *Great,* she thought.

"I've been wanting to introduce the two of you. Waiting, actually."

George poured Elizabeth a glass of wine from the bottle open on the counter. "He talks of little else."

"Dinner will be ready in minutes."

"Should I put dessert in the fridge? I made your favorite. Well, Casey did."

Kade smiled. He had the face of a kid in a candy shop. Someone for whom everything was turning out right. "I'm a lucky man, indeed."

"So, Elizabeth. Kade says you're a teacher in Story."

Where is this going? She cocked an eyebrow his way. "I am."

"She's a busy gal. Can hardly get a date with her myself."

"Since when is this?" Elizabeth thought of the past week, how absent Kade had been.

"I meant that when you're there, it's all hands on deck. You never say no." Kade sniffed at one pot, then replaced a lid. He withdrew a pan of garlic bread from the oven. With tongs, he tossed the slices into a napkin-lined basket.

Elizabeth wanted to be irked, but the scent made her stomach growl. She watched as he ladled pasta, then sauce, into bowls.

"Looks incredible," George said. "What can I carry?"

Kade handed him a large, wooden salad bowl. "Benny? How about you boys wash up and meet us in the dining room?"

A faint "Okay!" came from down the hallway followed by a sink shushing on.

Elizabeth sat on one side of the table, George on the other. She gave him a tight smile.

"Boys?" Kade sank into the seat at the head of the table. "Dinner's getting cold."

Benny made his appearance, hair wet and combed. Elizabeth guessed from Rhett's damp locks that he'd done the same for her son. *Adorable.*

Benny climbed into the seat between his uncle and great uncle. He tucked his napkin in his lap.

Rhett struggled with the chair height, and Elizabeth gave him a boost. As she tucked in his chair, she wondered if he'd eat spaghetti at Kade's the way he did at home. Sauce pasted everywhere. Forehead, counter, and clothes. Leia often ate more from the floor than made it to Rhett's mouth. Elizabeth hoped Brutus, Kade's dog, was nearby to help clean up.

When she wedged Rhett in place, the little boy noticed the other adult at the table.

"Donk," he said.

Uh oh. Elizabeth had never before wished for her son's usual silence.

Kade placed a bowl in front of Rhett at the same moment he'd spoken.

"Donk," Rhett said again, and pointed at George. "Donk man."

Kade frowned at Rhett, his own steaming bowl of pasta in hand. "What did he say?"

"I wasn't listening," Elizabeth said, at the same time George said, "Didn't hear him."

Elizabeth's voice faltered. "I was too distracted by this aroma. Can't wait to dig in."

Kade turned his gaze to George and knitted his brow. "How does he know you work at Burros?"

"He said dog," George said. "Not burro. Kids say all kinds of things."

"This kid doesn't." Kade worked his jaw. "You work with dogs *and* donkeys, so my question stands."

"Can't something be a coincidence?"

"To quote Sir Conan Doyle, the universe is rarely so lazy."

21

"SO...HE LEFT?"

Jo leaned against a fence post. She'd dropped by the school. As one of the board members, the door was always open for the sheriff's wife. She pushed down on the end of the teeter totter, bouncing it with her foot.

"Worse," Elizabeth said. She recounted the rest of the evening. "He cleaned the kitchen while we ate. He even offered me a to-go box for my cheesecake. What am I going to do? I was so dumb. So unforgivably dumb."

"Foolish yes, but unforgivable—no. He'll get over it. Might take some work on your part, though. And George's."

Elizabeth rested her head against the chain link. She'd kicked herself, a mental exercise, every other minute.

At Sunday Supper, Jo had tried to get the story from Elizabeth, but she'd kept her lips zipped. She couldn't lay her shame out in front of her brother and Clint.

"Stupid, stupid, stupid. I'm back to square one of self-loathing and regret."

"Not the goal of my visit," Jo said.

"So, you've got good news then?" Elizabeth reached for a distraction from her consequences. "I keep thinking if only I'd—"

Jo interrupted. "Clint is going to call you. Ask you to come in."

"Why does it feel like I'm being called to the principal's office?"

Jo pursed her lips. "In a way, you are."

Elizabeth pressed at her temples. "Well, whatever it is, I didn't do it. Unless it's lying to Kade, then I'm guilty. But I don't think that's against the law."

"They got a hold of Laney's CGM recording."

The present came back to Elizabeth, a cold, hard reality. "Her what?"

"Blood sugar monitor. Sure have come a long way since my aunt had one. Thing is, Laney's didn't show a spike in blood pressure. In fact, she'd been having a great week."

Elizabeth pinched the space between her brows. "Wait, so would the monitor show the heart attack?" After the memorial, Jo had told Elizabeth about the cardiac arrest. Cause of Death. Common—expected, in some cases. Heartbreaking but not newsworthy.

"I don't know the details," Jo said. "Clint needs to ask some questions."

Elizabeth thought of Laney. Live and in the flesh in front of them one minute, gone the next. She thought of Wallace's words. Loss. "Be ready. Got it."

Jo gave her a shallow smile and turned to go. She took a few steps before turning back. "Almost forgot," she said. "I've started collecting donations. Should be a decent haul. I know you said Casey had the food under control, but we still need music."

With the drama from that weekend, Elizabeth had forgotten about the event.

As Jo began to list the items donated so far, Elizabeth spotted George in his yard. The man held long-handled loppers with which he hacked at an overgrown cottonwood. "Let me handle the music. I think I have an idea."

22

ELIZABETH SET FOOT TO pavement after school. One boot in front of the other, she made a beeline for the house across the street.

A leaf blower rested on the front porch, its cord looped in a neat coil. Elizabeth stepped around the machine and knocked on the door. Three short raps.

George answered. Baseball played on a small, flatscreen television screen hung on the wall. On the coffee table sat a plate with half a ham and cheese sandwich abandoned on the teal ceramic.

"Wasn't expecting you," George said. "Come in."

Elizabeth shivered. She'd been so focused on her agenda she'd forgotten her coat in the break room.

George reached for a throw blanket draped over a chair. "I keep the thermostat down. Saves me buckets." He handed the blanket to her. "I'd wondered if our afternoons had come to a close."

"About that—"

"Nope, not interested. The only thing I wanted to say is that I didn't think you'd stop visiting because Kade's feelings were a little hurt. I guess I was wrong."

George picked up his abandoned sandwich to take a bite.

"It's a two-way street, you know."

"What's that?"

"Talking. Visiting. I always come here."

"So, we're friends now? Seemed like last week, I wasn't fit to do my job."

"I didn't mean—" George shot Elizabeth a look. She stopped, restarted. "I did say some things. Some awful things, and I'm sorry."

He nodded, as if to acknowledge without full acceptance.

"You're here now. And on time for the game."

Elizabeth gestured toward her car. "I can't stay. I've got to rescue my babysitter. She has a date with her husband. I'm pet sitting."

"Rain check, then," George said. It wasn't a question. He was a lot like his nephew, Elizabeth thought. Quiet, thoughtful, and stubborn as an ox.

"Before I go...I wanted to ask...since you're working at Burro Buddies and all..."

"Out with it."

"I was hoping you'd play at the fundraiser. Music."

"No."

"What? But...you haven't even heard—"

"I said no." George turned back toward the television.

"But you'll be there anyway, right? We had a band coming but they hand to cancel and—"

"Find another musician. I'm busy."

Elizabeth wanted to argue, to push him into her vision. She opened her mouth to reply when the crunch of tires on gravel announced the arrival of a car.

Swift, powerful knocks reverberated through the door, two beats later. When George opened it, Guy Henderson walked through.

"Love what you've done with the place, George." Guy strode in, the picture of male dominance. He wore a hunter green vest over a blue sweater. He clapped his brother on the shoulder. "Looks the same. Almost...homey."

George's eyes narrowed, and his hands balled into fists. "What are *you* doing here?"

"Can't a guy visit his long lost partner after his incarceration?"

"Most people learn from a young age not to go places where they aren't wanted."

"And here I thought the town's pariah would appreciate a visitor, though I see you've already got one." Guy looked Elizabeth up and down, then smirked.

"Don't know why you bothered to come," George said. "It's not like you visited me in prison. Now get out of my house."

Guy perused the room, stopping at the bowling trophies, the few pictures on the wall. "Now is that any way to treat me after all I've done for you?"

"You tried to sell my house!"

Guy stopped at the window looking out on the creek. He shrugged at the view. "It's nothing special."

"You were always jealous Dad left it to me." He poked a finger at Guy's chest, a jab for each word. "It ate you up."

"Bah," Guy said. He stepped back from George's contact. He ran his finger along the mantle. "Why would I need a shack? My place is four times the size. You should come and visit. We can dig out the old photo albums."

"I'm too busy putting my life back together. My own *family* put me in prison."

Guy clucked his tongue, a sound of pity. "Now, now. I thought you'd need the cash. You know, to start over."

"You mean you wanted to skim a cut off the sale," George spat. His venom for the other man was palpable. "I wouldn't have needed it if you hadn't framed me for your dirty work. You ruined *years* of my life so you could be free." George grabbed at his own hair and pulled, his face red and puffy. "I could kill you for what you did to me!"

Guy's response was icy, steady. "Someone had to protect the business. I seemed to be the only one willing to help us survive. Keep the cash flowing. Protect the family name."

"The only family member you protected was yourself."

Guy evaded his brother's barbs. He returned his attention to Elizabeth. "Already befriending Kade's uncle, I see. Skip right over his dear-ol'-dad."

Elizabeth stepped forward. She'd had enough. "As if I would have had anything to do with *you*."

Guy shook his head. "Pity. Might want to think twice about your choices. This family isn't exactly the warm and fuzzy type. Crooks and thieves, the lot of them. Might rub off on the small-town school teacher."

"Get. Out." George's voice was part warning, part threat. "Before I throw you out."

Guy flared his nostrils, as though considering a retort. Instead, he turned to Elizabeth. "A pleasure to see you again, Ms. Blau." He stalked out.

The screen door slammed behind him. Elizabeth waited for the sounds of the engine to fade into the distance before she spoke. "What was that about?"

George watched through the window as Guy's car disappeared down the road. "Guy hid things," he said. "Small things and big things. Somewhere, somehow, people's lives became a game to him. Even family."

Elizabeth regarded George. His cheeks had filled out, and his clothes hung better on his frame. His hair, a lank mop a month ago, was full and curly. There was a new rug on the floor. A set of colorful dishes in the drying rack. A fruit basket. George's life was coming back together, piece by piece.

George continued to watch the road, as if at any moment, Guy would be back. "He keeps things locked away, all for himself. Tries to be the puppet master. My guess about why he was here?" George's face darkened as he fixated on the empty road. "The bastard realized he's no longer the only one holding the strings."

23

FROM HER DOG BED, Leia uttered a soft growl. Elizabeth leapt up from the couch to open the door before a knock could wake Rhett.

Brutus bounded in ahead of Kade. Leia nosed her buddy and made room for him on the dog bed.

"I came as soon as I could. We've been slammed. Spent ten hours on this El Dorado. That job is going to have me working nights for a week," Kade said. When she looked behind him, he said, "Benny is staying at Marj's."

It was a quiet family rumor that Justin Hart, the man Elizabeth had dated for a brief moment in time last fall, may have been Benny's actual father. This would have made Marjory Hart, a wealthy ranch owner, his grandmother. Rather than test the theory, all parties were satisfied with regular visits. Marj got to be someone's Nana—a dream she thought had died with the death of her son—and Kade expanded the village that helped him raise his nephew like a son. Kade had decided that Benny could look into his genetics when—and if—he wanted.

"I'm so glad you're here," Elizabeth said, and threw herself into his arms.

Kade, stunned, embraced her, a slow and surprised gesture. "Me, too," he said. "Though I feel you are making this a little too easy."

Elizabeth leaned back from his broad chest. "Making what too easy?"

Kade loosened his grip around her waist and looked down at her. "My apologizing for the other night." He nudged his chin toward the bouquet he'd dropped on the doorstep when he caught her. "I even brought flowers."

Elizabeth looked down at the roses. Pink, again, and her new favorite. "What do you mean?"

"I was worried when you called. I thought you were going to tell me to take a hike. I panicked like anyone who'd acted like a jerk. I had a heart-to-heart with the mirror and then booked it over here to ask you to forgive me."

"Tell me more about the part where you were a jerk," Elizabeth said as she stooped to pick up the flowers, "while I put these in water. Then I'll tell you why I called."

Kade removed his hat and hooked it on the rack. "I was an idiot. I acted like a spoiled brat. In a weird way, I was jealous." He trailed after Elizabeth as she busied herself in the kitchen.

"Interesting that you should use that word..." Elizabeth snipped an inch off the bottom of each stem with sharp kitchen shears.

"Why is that?"

Elizabeth frowned at her arrangement. She reshuffled the stems. "That's coming up next. Keep going with the part where you're to blame."

Kade shoved his hand through his hair. "I don't know. I mean, it bugged me that y'all were hanging out together." Elizabeth made a face, and he was quick to continue. "Not in any weird way. I haven't had enough time with either one of you. I'm knee deep in my business and then withBenny, and...then to find out that you two were spending time together without me...It crushed me, Liz. Like if I couldn't keep up, life would go on without me."

"Motherhood in a nutshell," Elizabeth said, and stroked a petal. "Parenthood, I assume, but being a woman adds a layer."

"I'm learning that," Kade said. "Also—and this is selfish—I didn't like the idea of y'all having fun without me. Childish as hell, I know."

Elizabeth picked up the vase. It was blown glass, a piece of art. Filled with roses, it was stunning. "It is childish. Reminds me of a bento box, though."

"A what?" He followed her into the living room.

"Bento boxes. For packing your lunch? They usually have a couple different sections. Or like a tiffin tin. They have layers."

"You have a much fancier concept of lunch than I do. At the shop, we tend to get ours from a paper sack."

Kade's apology had eased the sting of the other night. The awkward goodbye. The look on Rhett and Benny's faces. Elizabeth continued. "A bento box keeps foods separate. Like you might want your veggies to stay out of the sauce until it's time to eat."

"Unlike Thanksgiving where I pile everything on one plate. I think I get it. It's like I didn't want the two of you to connect until I was ready."

Elizabeth scrunched up her forehead. "I had a cousin who used to stir everything together at Thanksgiving. It was gross. But yeah, that's what I meant. I need to apologize, too. We lied to you. To be fair, I didn't know he was your uncle when I met him. I thought he was someone new, and I was trying to be nice."

"He told me, and I appreciated his guilt, too. Still, my behavior wasn't fit for anyone's dining table. It won't happen again. You should spend time with whomever, whenever, without worrying about this brute."

The color drained from Elizabeth's face, and she took a deep breath. "Speaking of brutes..."

Kade was silent while she told him what she'd witnessed. His topaz eyes darkened into an amber tone as she shared what happened in George's living room. When she'd finished, he closed his eyes, then opened them again, a determined look on his face. He snatched his hat off the rack and jammed it down on his head. "I'll be right back."

"Wait! Where are you going?" Elizabeth asked the question to an empty living room.

He was already gone.

24

Elizabeth paced in the living room. She forged a path between the back door and the front door, checking each window at every pass. Casey had long since taken care of his goats and his bay roan and taken off for Danny's house. Elizabeth double-checked the locks and continued to worry.

Headlights on the horizon alerted her to Kade's return. She drew a shawl around her shoulders and ducked out the front door. What had dragged on like hours had been less than one.

To keep herself from running over to his truck and demanding news, Elizabeth tilted her head back to observe the stars. Glitter among the heavens, they made her feel small and cold. Her heart was heavy under the weight of so much space.

Kade spoke before she could demand an explanation. "He didn't answer."

"Who? Answer what?"

"My father," Kade said. "Guy. I knocked on the door—no, I pounded—and nothing. He was either asleep or pretending I wasn't there. Might have to apologize to his neighbors for the yelling."

Elizabeth furrowed her brow. "Yelling? I thought you said he wasn't there."

Kade crossed his arms. "In case he was there but hiding from me, I told him exactly what I think of him. Twice. I may have done so at top volume."

Elizabeth wondered what she would have said, and how she would have said it, if given the chance. Guy had treated her like scum, and she'd only known him for a few months. She imagined Kade's anger, stacked up over a lifetime.

"My uncle isn't perfect. Maybe he did some of the things they said he did. Or helped. Or turned a blind eye. I'm not sure how to know that. I can't know that. What I am certain of is that he never would have sold out his family. In fact, he risked his career, his relationship with his brother, to help me."

While Kade fumed, Elizabeth thought of George. She struggled to reconcile the man who cared for animals and loved oatmeal raisin cookies with the one at the open house. The one who'd threatened his brother with incredible fury.

"I should go," Kade said. He dragged his hand down his face as though to wipe the events from his memory. "This day has kicked my butt."

"It's late," Elizabeth said. "You'll plow into a deer, and then I'll be guilty for making you come all the way out here. You should just stay here." Kade looked at her, and his eyebrow twitched. Before his thoughts could drift further, she continued. "There's Casey's room, but he's kind of a slob. You'd never know it with how pristine the rest of the place looks. We've got a comfy couch, though," she added, before either of them could drum up other ideas.

Kade eyed the pile of cushions and the throw blanket. He yawned, a reflex. "I'll get up early and get out of your hair. That Chevy won't repaint itself."

Elizabeth extracted another blanket from the linen closet and handed it to Kade. "Maybe your father is already thinking of how to make things right with his brother. Might have already come back to apologize. Take him out for a beer."

"I hope you're right."

Kade was asleep the moment his head hit the pillows. Elizabeth was awake for long after that, doubting every word she'd said.

25

POUNDING ON THE DOOR roused Elizabeth from a deep sleep.

She'd been dreaming, and her head swam toward consciousness.

In her dream, she walked atop a fence line, balanced on the wire. One side was lava, the other a sea of people calling her name, reaching up to tug at her clothing. Her foot had slipped, and she was about to fall. To which side, she didn't know.

Awake and groggy, she glanced at Rhett. He lay curled up, still lost in his own dreamland.

The pounding sounded again. Elizabeth unhooked her robe from the door hook. She wrapped it around herself and tied the strap. Had Casey forgotten his key? The clock on her bedside table betrayed an early hour.

"I'm coming," she mouthed, when the knocking came again. She opened the door to slip out. As she did, she remembered Kade was in the living room—or had been. Had he locked himself out? She doubted either man would risk her wrath by waking Rhett.

Kade was already at the door. He stood there in his boxer shorts, Casey's shotgun at his side.

"Sheriff," he said when he opened the door. "Guessing you aren't bringing good news."

Elizabeth's heart sank. What happened—was it Casey? Or Jo?

She loathed these moments. They were the transitions between a peaceful place of ignorance to a new reality. A place where new information would cause pain in the best of cases and dire heartache in the worst. This was the wondering, a liminal space. Hope held hostage by logic.

A thousand worst-case scenarios streamed through her mind at once. The pressure, though short-lived, was so high she was grateful to have it end.

Then came the consequences.

Elizabeth rushed forward. "Who is it? What happened?"

"Ms. Blau, so sorry to disturb you. I am here for Mr. Michaels."

26

YOU LEARN MORE ABOUT retaliation on a playground than in a boardroom.

School is about people skills. If someone copies off your paper, you tell the teacher. Want a turn on the swings and some kid is being greedy? Push them off. Need to use the unbroken crayons? Take them. Coaches get teams pumped up to ensure victory against arch rivals. Parents compete with each other, like crabs in a bucket, to have their kid at the top of the class. It's even in the books they have you read. *Hamlet. The Count of Monte Cristo. Dune.*

They teach you about getting even in school—if you read between the lines.

It's even in math. If you take something from this side of the equal sign, the same is coming off the other side, one way or another.

It's the order of operations, simple as that.

What I've learned about revenge is the magic in waiting.

React too soon and you spoil the anticipation. You miss the opportunity to plan with detail. To savor execution.

When you get too itchy about it, let your trigger finger do the thinking, you might sacrifice the artistry. Miss a detail, a person, place, or thing that ties it all together.

Mr. Whitesell, my algebra teacher, said a thing worth doing is worth doing right the first time.

Revenge isn't for the impatient.

I made a list, you see. To bide my time.

If a person starts picking up rocks, you find a lot of creepy crawlies underneath. The more rocks, the more pests.

When you start to take apart a situation, let yourself get into the thick of what went wrong and who is to blame, you realize that it's nuanced. Layered.

It's easy to blame the teacher for assigning homework. Rarely does a kid blame the school board for the course load. Their parents for the choice in neighborhoods. Themselves for being lazy, sloppy.

Revenge requires critical thinking. You don't have to have money, fame, or a bikini body. You need to be able to dissect what happened down to its core. Let it crawl up inside your brain and take root. Only when you can feel what happened will you come back at it with the depth required to shake foundations.

If you're going to strike a match, might as well burn the whole damn bridge to the ground. Get granular. End the conflict at DNA level.

Anyone can get even in the moment. It takes a true player to make it count.

That's where I'm at.

I've had years to sit on the past, lug it around with me.

Now, I'm using what I've learned. Settling the score.

27

ELIZABETH RAN GLASSES THROUGH the washer, refilled pretzel bowls, and wiped down a half dozen tables. Each time she tuned back in to the chatter of customers, the fire remained the topic on everyone's lips.

"The whole place went up like a pile of pine needles."

"Someone told me it's still smoldering."

"How'd it happen? Must have been electrical. Can't trust a contractor these days."

"They'll figure it out. Poor bastard."

"Don't you mean who?" Big Ricky held a glass to his lips. He paused to comment before taking a sip. "We all know he didn't have friends and collected enemies like baseball cards."

"Easy there, Rick. Those are big accusations to sling around. This isn't one of those mafia shows you watch."

The crew at their bar stools continued their debate, voices rising.

Buzz brought in a box of Maximum Brewing T-shirts. At the shelves, he checked labels and rolled each shirt into a tight bundle.

Big Ricky called to him. "What do you think, Buzz? Accident or intentional?"

Buzz tucked the shirts on shelves according to size. Elizabeth thought of Casey's designs for Blau Brewing. One day she'd stack her own shirts. Hats, too.

"My mother raised me to never speak ill of the dead. No matter their sins. Brings bad luck."

Big Ricky and the others pressed Buzz, but he waved them off.

Elizabeth ignored their idle gossip as she ran through the tabs and refilled empties. When she turned to set a full pint on the counter in front of Ricky's buddy, a John Deere salesman whose name rhymed with gone—Don? Tom? John? Elizabeth couldn't remember—Ira took an empty stool and perused the menu.

"The lady brewer," he said.

"Hello there. Back for our latest release?"

Ira gave her a half smile. "That and to see if you've thought about my offer." He looked over each shoulder. "Though the crowd is entertaining today."

Elizabeth shook her head. "They think of themselves as some kind of mystery-solving gang at this point. Makes me tired."

She had thought of his offer. Was thinking about it every moment. An investor meant she could have her own brewery. Not in ten years, now. Ira had used the term silent partner. How silent would that be?

Elizabeth was tempted but torn. A deal meant she would still owe her existence, her survival, to the generosity of a man.

"I've thought about it some. But a few things came up. Personal life stuff," Elizabeth said. She thought of Kade and their relationship. She wasn't sure if she could afford a house or a stake in a brewery but definitely couldn't do both. What did she want more?

"I'm a good listener. Comes with the territory."

Big Ricky interrupted before Elizabeth could speak, his words slurred at the edges. "It's her father-in-law who was the victim. In the fire."

"Guy is not—was not—my father-in-law," Elizabeth said.

Big Ricky held a hand to his chest. "Soon to be, I would've put money on it. Still, he's gone now. God rest his soul."

Buzz rescued Elizabeth. "Enough, Ricky. Regardless of what happened to Guy, Kade is here, and he's a friend of ours. He's got to clean up after the whole mess. His girlfriend doesn't need to hear a constant stream of gossip. Let them get through this. Enough. Everyone."

Buzz shot a look around the room, as though daring anyone to resuscitate the topic.

Ricky held up both hands as if to decry his innocence. "I beg your pardon, Elizabeth," he said. "My mouth gets away from me sometimes."

Elizabeth gave him an imperceptible nod and turned back to Ira.

Ira's face was slack. He had a little smile at the corner of his lips, curious. "You're Kade's girlfriend?"

"I am. Do you know him?"

"I did. A long time ago, though. Worked on one of my cars." He set some bills by his glass and pushed back from the bar.

Elizabeth frowned as she watched him leave.

"You can't make everyone happy," Buzz said behind her.

What did I say?

28

"MS. BLAU, THANK YOU for coming in."

Sheriff Wolf took a seat behind his desk. He shuffled a few papers until he unearthed his pen from beneath the layers.

"Will you ever start calling me Elizabeth?"

"At work? Nope." Wolf opened one desk drawer and extracted a small recording device.

Elizabeth sighed. "You could serve better coffee in the waiting room. Makes me second guess my compliance."

Wolf shrugged, then scribbled his pen on a pad of paper to get the ink to flow. "Been drinking it for decades at this point. Why change now?"

"I've got an hour before Beans closes to correct my mistake."

The sheriff lifted his eyebrows, pressed his lips together, and then looked down at his notes. "I'm going to record if that's okay with you?"

"Go ahead," Elizabeth said.

Sheriff Wolf pressed a button and cleared his throat. He detailed the meeting date and time, the people present, and asked for her consent. When she acknowledged him, he began.

"Thank you for coming down here today of your own accord."

"Am I being investigated?"

Wolf ignored her question. "To begin, let's start with Melanie Horowitz."

"Start with?"

"Can you please tell me the last time you saw her alive?"

Elizabeth shifted her position in the office chair. The green plastic was stiff. "The one and only time I saw her was on the South Piney Trail with Jo Wolf. I assume you are familiar with her?"

Elizabeth glanced at Wolf. His face didn't flinch. She continued with the details of their meeting, down to the time, the weather, and what Laney was wearing.

"And you saw no signs of distress? No bruising or other injuries?"

"No." Elizabeth thought of the woman, spry and capable, walking with purpose. "She was maybe a little—distracted? She said something about getting on to dinner."

Wolf nodded, checked that the recorder was still on, and continued. "Thank you. Only a few more questions."

Elizabeth wondered what Laney's monitor indicated to turn a heart attack into an inquiry. Had someone hurt her? How could the data show that?

"Who found Laney?"

Wolf ignored her question. He flipped over the sheet in his notepad to a fresh page. "Can you please tell me the last time you saw Guy Henderson alive?"

A tingling sensation zipped between Elizabeth's shoulders. Her scalp flashed hot.

George's voice rang in her ears. *Get. Out.*

"The other afternoon. Wednesday."

"Where was this?"

Elizabeth clutched the arms of the office chair in which she sat. Her knuckles whitened. "George Henderson's house. In Story."

Wolf scribbled on the pad, his face unmoving. "Why were you there?"

"We're friends. Well...friendly. Anyway, I stopped by to say hello—"

"Do you stop by often?"

What could this mean? What is Clint getting at? "He lives across the street from my work. He's my boyfriend's uncle. I stop by a couple of times a week, I guess."

"Go on." Wolf watched her, pen at the ready.

"That day, Guy came over."

Wolf prodded further. "And then what happened?"

Elizabeth's mouth was dry, her nerves playing havoc on her speech. Separating Sheriff Wolf from the Clint she knew was difficult in the best of times. Today it was torturous.

"I...uh...they...well..."

"Ms. Blau? Please continue when you are ready." His eyes flicked to his wall clock.

Elizabeth checked the time herself. She clasped her hands and squeezed. The truth was the truth, no matter what—right? With a deep breath, she steadied herself, then told Wolf as much as she could remember from that afternoon.

"I see," he said when she'd finished. "And how did Mr. Michaels react when you told him this?"

Elizabeth looked up. *How did he know I told Kade?* Not only was George wrapped up in this, but now Kade was. Her stomach twisted, and she fought the urge to jump up and run for the door. Wolf's line of questioning meant one thing: they were looking for someone on whom to pin Laney and Guy's deaths. George and Kade were tied to that search somehow.

"He wasn't happy. He left to go talk to his father."

"Guy." When Elizabeth nodded, Wolf continued. "Can you tell me when he left and when he came back?"

Elizabeth gave him the details of that night, up until when Kade went to sleep. "The next thing I knew, you were pounding on the door at an ungodly hour, and here we are."

"Did Mr. Michaels have a weapon with him?"

"With him?"

"As in, did he take a weapon with him to Mr. Henderson's house?"

"Not that I know of. Why?"

"Thank you, Ms. Blau, that will be all. For now."

29

SEVERAL HEADS DIPPED OVER the edge of the corral. Two horses and a mule nuzzled each other, jostling to get a better view of the new arrivals.

"Donk," Rhett said. At almost three years old, he still preferred his single syllable versions of words. Elizabeth cringed at the reminder of the night at Kade's and that one little word.

"Pretty sure that one is a mule, buddy. Two horses and one mule. Friends," Elizabeth said. She hoisted Rhett up to get a closer look at the mule.

The speech therapist had warned them against mirroring anything similar to baby talk. Elizabeth assured the woman there was no way a science teacher was into baby talk—unless it was to tell Leia she was the very best dog. Because whatever the occasion, she was.

For her part, Leia hopped out of the car. She was welcomed at Rhett's therapy sessions, her attendance encouraged by the therapist. First, the stuffy woman considered Leia a four-legged coach since she'd inspired his first word.

Leia also buddied up to Corbin's dogs, like an unpaid intern. The big sandy-colored dog circled the pens and enclosures, romped in the runs with the other pups, and navigated the place with authority. Corbin knew that animals comfortable around other animals had a better chance of adoption.

"Come on, girl," Elizabeth said. "No getting muddy, this time."

Elizabeth steered Rhett toward the llamas. They'd ended last week's session there, and the therapist thought they'd made progress. L-sounds were typical for three-year-olds, and she'd used the llamas to introduce the sound. Elizabeth wanted to provide the proper pronunciation—with a Y sound—but Casey told her to keep quiet. He'd said that sometimes her penchant for facts wasn't helpful.

She held off. For now.

One other car had occupied the tidy gravel lot when they arrived. Elizabeth recognized it as the therapist's. A sleek, silver sedan befitting the trim, silver-haired woman who drove it.

"Hello there," Dr. Hawthorne said. "How are we today?"

Elizabeth wanted to respond that her boyfriend's father died, she had big dreams to go with a small bank account, and she had a massive fundraiser to plan. *Everything is just peachy, thanks.* Instead, she said, "We're good."

Dr. Hawthorne smiled, a Cheshire cat. "Wonderful." She turned her back to Elizabeth. "Rhett, I'm so glad you could meet me by the llamas today."

Ya-mas, Elizabeth thought. With a sigh, she headed for the shelter of the barn. A chilly wind whipped through the enclosures, and the tall structure would block it. *Should I have put on Rhett's gloves? Too late now.*

Elizabeth wandered toward the shelter's handful of buildings. He'd built each facility with massive solar panels on every roof. The chicken coop was no exception. Its tiny windmill turned a quick rotation in the wind.

Inside, Corbin had styled the coop like a dovecote. Rows of nooks gave each bird a nesting spot. She stroked the few chickens who appreciated her touch and gave the others their space. A few birds resettled themselves. In this quiet place, their dozens of heartbeats sheltered together.

A fat raindrop spattered Elizabeth's cheek when she exited the warm coop. More fell on the ground, a polka dot pattern.

She scurried toward the big barn as the skies opened up.

Elizabeth ran for the small office at the side of the building. She assumed the session would move inside. Instead of her son and the therapist, she found Hannah Black.

Hannah sat in a folding chair, tapping on her phone. "If you're looking for Corbin, get in line. George said he's out.

Ran to get some more feed from somewhere. There's a peacock now, did you know that?" The woman rolled her eyes as though she expected Elizabeth to commiserate.

Elizabeth saw no one else in the office. "I'm actually looking for my son and his doctor. Did they come in here?"

Hannah shrugged.

Elizabeth was halfway out the door to look for them when Hannah's voice plied her back.

"I heard about what happened. The fire. That's one messed up family. Good looking, though." When she saw the glare on Elizabeth's face, Hannah continued. "Don't worry, it was only once and not with your boyfriend. Not for lack of trying on my part, though."

Elizabeth wanted to snap at Hannah. There was a bitter taste in her mouth, venom at the tip of her tongue. Instead, she zipped her lips and stormed out.

30

"DON'T LET HER GET to you. Did you find Rhett?"

"Would I be here with you if I hadn't?"

The women wound through the aisles of the grocery store. Jo pushed the cart while Elizabeth hunted inspiration.

"Hannah wanted to get under your skin. It's like a game."

"I know that, but I don't want to play." Elizabeth stopped at a box of graham crackers. "Can you believe the ingredient list on these things? Homemade is a thousand times better. Hey, what if we did s'mores by a fire pit?"

Jo leaned her forearms on the cart handle. "Have you seen a fire pit at the shelter?"

"Plan B, then. We're going to have loads of apples and pears. Maybe cobbler? Individual servings. We could pull out ice cream."

They moved from the baking aisle into produce. "Why don't you want to talk about why Hannah bugs you?"

"She doesn't bug me," Elizabeth said. She disbelieved her words the moment they left her mouth. "Okay, so she does bother me. It's the way she acts. Like she won a prize and wants to remind me at every turn."

"Prizes are in the eyes of the beholder," Jo said. She hefted a bag of apples. She held them up and said, "Cobbler?"

"You're onto something there."

Jo steered the cart around a box of late season corn. "With the dish or the jealousy?"

"Can we drop the Hannah topic if I say both?"

Jo stifled a smile.

"What if we did a chili cook off? We could sell taster tickets. Raffle off new slow cookers. Get people involved in the fundraiser. Then we could focus our efforts on sides and desserts."

"I like this idea. Very fall-like."

Elizabeth hefted a mango. "We could also highlight the local ingredients, make it farm-to-table."

"I am always in for a challenge. Some people will fudge a bit, but I like the plan."

Elizabeth crossed her arms to hold opposite elbows. She turned a slow circle in the store, taking in the illusion of plenty. "I need to plan."

"I'm a fan of anything that involves lists," Jo said. "I also think it's brilliant to monetize the meal. Tickets are perfect. It gives everyone a theme for the auction baskets. We might actually pull this off."

"I could use a win," Elizabeth said. They reached the check-out lines. She placed her milk, baking powder, and a bag of oranges on the counter. "This has been a week I wouldn't want to relive."

"How is Kade doing?"

Elizabeth tucked her purchases into her reusable sack and shouldered the bag. "As well as can be expected for someone whose estranged father was incinerated in a house fire." She shuddered. "Even saying it is horrible."

Jo's phone chirped from inside her purse. She fished it out and glanced at the incoming text. "Without revealing more than I'm allowed to, I think it would be a good idea to swing by the garage on your way home."

31

ELIZABETH HELD A TO-GO cup from Beans in each hand, her usual dirty chai in one and coffee, black, in the other. She lifted alternating fingers on each hand to redistribute the concentration of heat.

With her hip, Elizabeth bumped the car door shut. Eyes on the sidewalk, she heel-toed her way forward. Gary had filled each cup to the brim, and she didn't want to spill a drop. More than the potential for burns, coffee was next to sacred in a teacher's book.

At the door marked Pull, Elizabeth paused. How to open it with hands full was an issue. More pressing, though, was the explanation of her presence.

How to justify her sudden arrival? Stopping by the garage wasn't part of her typical girlfriend actions. Kade's Garage wasn't on the way to her work or home. He was busy more work days than not, and she never wanted to bug him. Random coffee was a weak offering.

It wasn't that she hadn't tried to reach out. Since the news swept the county, Kade drew inward. She could only imagine the questions, the attempt at helpful statements. The looks.

As her arms tired and she debated whether to head home, Alma came to her rescue. The mechanic held the door for her friend.

"Thanks," Elizabeth said. "I'm sorry I didn't bring you anything."

"S'alright. I'm on edge as it is working with the poor guy this week. He gives dark and brooding a run for its money." Alma whispered the last comment under her breath as she nudged her chin toward the bays. "If any more of the 'well-meaning' stop by to pump him for information, I'm going to turn the power hose on them." She raised both her eyebrows at Elizabeth. "Good luck."

Elizabeth peeked back out to the parking lot. No sheriff—yet.

Kade was in the corner of the shop, tearing through a massive tool chest.

"Hello there," Elizabeth said. "Looking for something?"

"No. Yes. Ugh." Kade sighed and turned around. He flung up his hands in defeat. "This place is falling to pieces. Nothing is where it should be. I've got to reorganize all of it, top to bottom, at this rate."

Elizabeth held out the cup of coffee. "Fuel for the work?"

Kade took the cup. He sniffed at the lip before taking a sip. "Somehow you knew what I needed. Thank you."

"Jo and I were planning for the fundraiser at Beans. She says hello, by the way, and wants me to bug you for a donation. We're doing an auction."

"Put us down for a year of oil changes. That's our usual. Raj will make up a certificate when he gets back. He's got the best handwriting out of all of us."

"How's his vacation going?"

"Sent me a picture of a massive salmon. Said he had a cedar plank ready for the barbecue. More weekends with a rod and reel in hand seems to suit his recovery."

In her periphery, Elizabeth saw Sheriff Wolf's cruiser enter the lot and park at the side of the building. Elizabeth looked at Kade.

He hadn't missed the new arrival and watched the last bay whose door yawned open a few feet. The sheriff's boots were visible before the man himself ducked under.

Under his breath, Kade said, "This can't be good."

"Mr. Michaels. Ms. Blau."

"Sheriff," Kade said, and nodded. "How are the highways?"

"Quiet today, which is a blessing." The sheriff removed his hat and turned the brim between his hands. He looked at Elizabeth and then back at Kade, as if to ask if her presence was okay. Kade shrugged, so he continued. "I'm sorry I don't come with more news about what happened. The investigation is ongoing."

A twitch under Kade's right eye gave away the reaction boiling below the surface. He nodded at Wolf, a sign to continue.

"It's clear that you are next of kin. Some of his...assets will be tied up a bit longer, but I know his lawyer will be in touch. He said you've talked?"

Kade nodded, a surprise to Elizabeth. She didn't know Kade had already been in talks with the lawyer.

"We recovered a box from the house. I got it cleared to hand over. Seems like it was under some floorboards in a sort of a custom storage spot."

The sheriff held out a box. It was overlaid with detailed carvings. Colorful, it was out of place in the mechanic's realm.

"Sign here, and it's yours."

Kade pulled a pen from his coverall pocket and signed the form Wolf handed him. Wolf traded the box for the paperwork, and Kade gave the container a little shake.

"They had to take a look. Photograph the items, you know."

Kade opened the box and extracted a handful of papers, rolled in a tube. He shuffled toward the closest table with a shop light overhead. With a tug on the chain, he illuminated the contents of the box.

"Deeds?"

"Seems like it," Wolf said. He hooked his thumbs into his belt loop and remained in place. Elizabeth didn't know if she was wanted and didn't want to go if she was. She stayed put, eager to see what Kade examined in the light.

Kade extracted a picture of a little boy, straddling a tricycle. He had a bowl cut, a striped shirt, and white tennis shoes. He could have been any kid on a suburban street, but Elizabeth would have recognized those honey-colored eyes anywhere.

Wolf stayed quiet while Kade stared into the photograph. After a minute, he set it aside and turned back to the box. Elizabeth spotted a tear sliding down his jawline.

At the bottom of the box was a key. It dangled from a small tag with a bank's name stamped on the side. "Safety deposit box?"

Wolf nodded. "If it had been in his name, we would have opened it."

"But it isn't," Elizabeth said, catching up. "It's under Kade's."

Kade drew his eyebrows together. "But I don't..." His protest faded.

"We hoped you might know what's inside."

"I didn't even know I had an account, I would have no idea where to...oh."

Elizabeth and Wolf waited.

"First Bank of Sheridan."

"How do you know?" Sheridan was small, but it had more than one bank. "We had to hunt that down. Shop the key around."

"A birthday present. When I turned ten, I was given my own savings account with a hundred dollars in it," he said. "Never mind where it came from, I was to build something great with it."

"Laney," Elizabeth whispered.

Kade nodded. "That was my guess. She handled everything for Guy, down to his bank accounts."

Elizabeth put a hand on Kade's shoulder. A faraway look had settled in his eyes. She considered the key in his hand and the picture on the table. "Want me to go with you?"

"I can't ask that," he said. "It's my rotten family drama."

Wolf stepped in. "My advice? Let her be there for you. We weren't meant to go through hard things alone."

32

"WHEN ARE YOU GOING over there?"

Elizabeth and Jo dug through a bin at The Golden Goose. Part thrift store, part vintage treasure trove, the shop was crammed with everything from forty-eight-star American flags to boxes of gaudy costume jewelry. Floor-to-ceiling shelves staged into booths directed customers through a warehouse of items.

They pawed through a display of table decorations. Jo wanted sunflowers in tiny vases, checkered prints. On a shoestring budget, they needed to find deals.

"Tomorrow after work," Elizabeth said. "Clint told him to please keep him informed if Kade found anything of interest. Sounds like they're fishing for something."

"Sounds about right," Jo said. "Got to have probable cause and all that."

Elizabeth held up a tool that looked like a wooden whale vertebra. "They want ten bucks for this? I'm not even sure what it does."

Jo paused her search through a stack of fabric. "Horse hame," she said. "Half of one, anyway."

"Which is a...what, exactly?"

"Picture the other half forming a U of sorts. It's part of a big harness. Distributes the load." Jo mimed wrapping her neck with what appeared to be a heavy scarf.

"Like a backpack frame," Elizabeth said. She flipped the piece around in her hand.

"Same concept. So, Kade has no idea what's in the box?"

Elizabeth teased. "I figured you would have peppered Clint with all these questions. Wifely privilege and all."

Jo shrugged. "I prefer the source. Clint forgets all the little details and gets frustrated when I ask him for more." Jo affected a deep, booming voice. "Good gravy, Jo, you know I don't have your memory."

Elizabeth laughed, releasing tension. The last week had been a flurry of hard news, halted plans, and limbo.

Jo continued, "If the fire report has anything fishy in it, they'll regret every stone they didn't turn over."

Elizabeth paused before a shelf of smaller vases. Different sizes and shapes, they made an eclectic collection. She picked up a small blue one and held it up to the light. "Kade said it could take weeks. Not sure if that bothers him or not, though. He's kind of hard to read."

"Kade Michaels? The strong and silent, no-nonsense, tall, dark, and handsome car mechanic? Can't see that at all."

Elizabeth made a face at Jo, then held out the vase. "What do you think of these? We could put one on each table. Tie raffia ribbon around them and fill them with colorful flowers."

"I can get behind that," Jo said. "Let's see if they have enough." She started counting the tiny vessels, tapping each with a fingertip.

Jo was at twenty-two when Elizabeth asked, "What do you think happened at Guy's house that night?"

"When an answer is on its way, I don't focus too much on guessing the outcome. I prefer to plan for what comes after."

33

ELIZABETH KNOCKED TWICE, THEN stepped back. While she waited, she'd taken in the yard and the subtle shifts along the property.

George, with help from Kade, had revived the tiny cabin she remembered from the open house. A thick boot mat greeted visitors at the door on which a wreath of conifer branches welcomed all inside. The carport, too short for his truck, had become wood storage. A cord of logs nestled in tight formation between anchored supports. He'd backed the rack with a sheet of siding to keep the weather off.

Beyond the cement slab, dead branches and debris were gone. A few trees had cut limbs, branches tamed back from the house. While the yard remained carpeted in pine needles, the cones had been collected and bagged. The old bench had been stripped and resealed. It gleamed in the afternoon light.

The once abandoned cabin was now inhabited and looked as though it would stay that way for seasons to come. She wanted the same for the man inside and had a plan to make it happen—if only he would answer the door.

She scuffed the toe of her boot against the mat, tamping down impatience. For her idea to work, she was running low on options.

George opened the door, a kitchen towel over one shoulder. "Hadn't seen you in a while." Their last interaction, the explosive visit by Guy, hung between them in the brisk autumnal air.

Elizabeth blinked, caught off guard. "I...uh...didn't want to get in the way of you and Kade. Then it was awkward with him, then with what happened..."

"With what happened..." George waited for her to finish.

Elizabeth pressed her hand to her cheek. She wasn't doing sympathy well. George had lost a brother. One with whom he'd had a brittle fight the day before the man's death, but still. "They say it takes six hundred milliseconds for a thought to go from your brain to your mouth. I need to slow mine down."

George regarded her a moment. His face was expressionless, as though he weighed his response, then broke the silence. "I've got a batch of sourdough rolls straight from the oven. My parole officer suggested I pick up some indoor hobbies before winter sets in. So far, I've taken up bread baking. It's not easy at this altitude."

"I've learned this myself."

"I've also got hot coffee and fresh butter." He swept his hand inward toward the kitchen. "How about you come in and teach me more about neurology?"

Shame flooded her thoughts at his ready invitation. Elizabeth hadn't reached out—until she needed something. She'd made a new friend only to ditch him when life got intense. How could she defend herself to people like her co-workers when she let her own assumptions get in the way? She followed him inside, her conscience twisted in guilt.

George poured coffee from a pot into two chipped mugs. Hers was emblazoned with the Cornhuskers logo on the side. She took a sip of the steaming liquid and let it warm her from within. George handed her a hot roll on a paper towel. It had a slit on top into which he'd slid a pat of butter to melt.

"Smells incredible," she said.

He nodded. "Take a bite. Tell me what you think of the rolls. Then tell me why you finally came by."

Elizabeth bit into the roll. The thin crust crackled and gave way to pillowy soft insides. She closed her eyes to savor the bite. "Heaven."

George nodded. "Okay, part one accomplished. Now for the ask."

"Why does it have to be an ask?"

"It isn't an ask?"

Sheepish, Elizabeth took another bite to give herself time to think. She swallowed, then fessed up. "It is an ask. I keep thinking back to your talent, the way you played the banjo, and I—"

"Nope," George said.

"Hear me out," Elizabeth said. "Please? You could play whatever you—"

"Not doing it."

"But—"

"You said it only takes three nanoseconds or whatever to say what you think. I must be ahead of the curve."

"I heard a gift," she said. Before he could utter a protest, she continued. "Who cares where you learned to play? You're amazing. That kind of skill deserves an audience. Why keep it all tucked away where only you and the squirrels can hear it?'

"That's just it. See, I don't play for anyone else now. I play for me. In fact, I don't plan to so much as eat when someone else tells me to. I earned my freedom back, and I'll be damned if I am forced into anything ever again.

Elizabeth opened her mouth to respond, saw the fire in his eyes, and decided to stay quiet. She took another sip of coffee and wadded up her paper towel.

"You know, my mom took up crochet," she said. "Not anything like what she did before. But where she's at, there are only so many options."

"I suppose you're going to tell me where she's at?"

"Prison. In Washington State. Will be for the foreseeable future."

Elizabeth gave George a rundown of her childhood. The escalating fights, Casey leaving when she was eight, and the tragic events that left her to live with an aunt and uncle to finish high school.

"Wait, your mom is in the state penitentiary for defending herself against her abuser, and y'all live here where you can't even visit?"

Elizabeth folded the paper towel into a smaller square. "It's not that simple," she said to the wad in her hand.

She had thought about visiting but found an excuse every time. Her aunt and uncle had taken her as a kid, but how long had that been? Guilt trickled into Elizabeth's subconscious as she scrambled for an explanation.

"I'll tell you what's simple. Showing up for people you care about. Not just when you need something. And definitely not just when you are trying to make yourself feel better."

34

A DRIZZLE LEFT STREAKS in the dust on Elizabeth's car. The rain dripped from her bumper and made a neat line in the dirt below. Wet leaves shimmered under their weight. She sat in the driver's seat as faint drops became a true rain, washing her windshield on repeat. *At least it isn't snowing,* she thought.

Elizabeth waited in Guy Henderson's driveway. She'd promised to meet Kade, to help him sift through his father's belongings.

In the car, rivulets striping the window, Elizabeth wasn't sure how to be of help. Further, waiting in front of the charred structure was anything but comforting.

At the brewery, whispers indicated a building reduced to ashes. Stories expanded to include a total clearance of land and structures, as though a fire had ripped through and left little in its wake.

In reality, the damage was incomplete. While the left half of the house appeared untouched, a thrown newspaper at the front door, the right side was in dramatic contrast. Glass littered the once immaculate lawn where the windows had blown from blackened frames. The siding, what little remained, had peeled and blackened, strips curled outward. The roof collapsed inward, gutters twisted on the ground. Smoke lingered in the air. Catastrophe and ruin. An ending. Destruction.

Headlights appeared in Elizabeth's side mirror. Kade's truck slid into the spot next to her car. His engine idled, the beams shining a faint arc on the garage doors.

When Kade didn't get out of the vehicle, Elizabeth grabbed her purse. She exited her car and reached for Kade's door handle. Rain pelted her face as she climbed into the cab.

Door closed, Elizabeth squeegeed her hair onto the floor mat. Kade stared at the house in front of him.

"I may have to row home," Elizabeth began, willing her heart to slow its patter. "The average person can only paddle at a speed of three miles per hour, though. I'd still be home for dinner. Maybe."

Elizabeth risked a peek at Kade. He hadn't moved. She bit her lip and matched his gaze. Guy's house loomed in front of them. The depression of the task ahead, no matter how brief, sank onto her lap like a lead weight. She reached for his hand and held it.

After a few minutes, Kade said, "Thank you."

"Of course." Elizabeth squeezed his hand.

Kade continued, "I've started to deal with some things. His things. The man had more stuff than I know what to do with. Land all over the place. A different lawyer calls me every day. The people at his company too. I'm getting my own lawyer to deal with the whole mess."

"There's an incredible unfairness in that."

Kade looked at her, his cheeks ashen. "I failed, Liz."

Elizabeth shook her head. "Failed what? You couldn't have known this would happen. Couldn't have pictured—this." She gestured to the rain-soaked remains in front of them. "You can't fail at something that wasn't your fault."

"Benny. I failed Benny." Kade covered his mouth with one hand and closed his eyes.

"I don't understand."

"When Polly...I mean he'd already had it so hard..."

Kade struggled to explain. On the seat between them, Elizabeth spotted a large manilla envelope from First Bank, a receipt stapled to its front.

"I vowed to keep him away from family drama. He didn't deserve the hand he was dealt. They put me in charge of his future. Charged me with this perfect boy. I was supposed to be the strong, calm influence. An uncle who had a stable life to share."

"You've given Benny an awesome life. He loves you." Elizabeth struggled for words that didn't stem from a greeting card.

"The problem is I'm not in any place to be someone's father. Look at what happened to mine." Kade held his hands out to the house, as though it represented the entirety of his relationship with Guy.

"Benny will know this was out of your control. This had nothing to do with you."

Kade turned toward her. "You know what to do for Rhett. Your whole household is a safe place. Y'all have healed, moved forward from your past. I'm still a mess. My problems are growing by the day." His voice held a bitter edge.

A few remaining roof tiles clattered to the cement, and Elizabeth flinched. "If this is too much, let's go. We can always come back another time."

Kade shook his head, then held her gaze. "He was shot, Liz. A single bullet to his skull."

35

"WOLF CALLED ME." He looked down at the steering wheel. "Execution style, he said. Single bullet. It's all in the report."

Elizabeth's lip trembled. "You mean...?"

"He was murdered."

Elizabeth was silent, pinned by his words.

"Somehow a horrible father I avoided like the plague he was is better than...a dead one."

Elizabeth's mind raced. Someone had killed Guy then covered it up with fire? "Did Wolf say they had any leads?"

Kade shook his head. "Who wasn't his enemy? You met the man."

Elizabeth spun her thoughts until her stomach soured. She looked back at the house, stark and empty, tattered and blackened. The darkened structure took on a sinister shadow.

Without warning, the truck cab opened. Kade, droplets splattering the arm of his jacket, said, "Let's get this over with before I change my mind."

Elizabeth blinked, a hesitation, before opening her own door to slide out of the vehicle. She ran to catch up with Kade. Instead of heading for the front door, he'd rounded the house to the backyard.

Behind Guy's house was a sizable workshop. Manufactured to mimic a barn, the spotless building had no sign of animal occupation. A corral, a small, unused patch, was spotless, its oval raked in neat lines. Crime scene tape still clung to the back porch.

Kade strode toward the workshop. In one hand, he held an envelope, its surface darkening with spots. At the door, he tore the seal and removed a small key ring from among the paperwork stuffed inside. He inserted the larger key into the lock and turned. Before she reached the doorstep, he'd pushed his way inside.

Elizabeth followed and pulled the door shut. Inside, the room pounded with sound. Rain beat against the metal roof, a percussion that drowned out their footsteps.

Kade reached for the light switch. Banks of fluorescent bulbs brightened the vast room.

In front of them sat a row of pristine machines: a drill press, a table saw, a lathe. There was a draftsman's desk, a work bench, and a massive gun safe.

Guy had filled his workshop with a riding lawn mower, a quad, a snowmobile, and a vintage tractor, the latter in spotless condition.

Goosebumps rose on Elizabeth's arms as they toured this museum of Guy's hobbies. She kept close to Kade as he made a beeline for the man-sized safe.

At the drafting table, he dumped out the contents of the envelope to fish for another set of keys. Ring in hand, he flipped through a few of the smaller keys, considering the lock.

While he debated, Elizabeth examined the plans draped over the table. Guy's notes and sketches spread across the massive desk, haphazard. In one sketch, he'd designed a tent that would set up its frame with the push of a button.

Elizabeth said, "Looks like he was into camping."

"He isn't. Wasn't." Kade glanced over her shoulder. "Not an outdoors kind of person. Likely some other way to defraud people. Spy on them, or something worse."

Cords dangled where a computer would have been. A monitor, its screen black, was mounted to the wall above. "What all did they take?"

"The killer or the police? Honestly, I have no idea. Wolf said it didn't look like a typical burglary. His wallet, car, laptop, and everything else was in the house. The cops have that. There's no way to know, or at least no way for me to know, if anything was taken. Not that it matters."

Kade was back at the safe. He inserted a key into the lock.

"You going to tell Wolf what you find?"

"Depends on what it is." Kade swung the heavy door open. Racks of weapons lined the interior. Many were vintage, their hand-carved stocks gleaming.

"What will you do with all of those?"

Kade pulled out his phone and turned on the flashlight. He shone it into the safe. "Get them appraised. That envelope or one of the dozen others he left behind likely has the paperwork. Figure it'll take me weeks to sort out. Then I'll sell them. Or most of them."

Kade grunted and withdrew a wooden box from deep within the safe. A memory pressed at Elizabeth as she watched him brush dust off the top of the box and set it on the table before lifting the lid.

A pair of matching impressions sank into the velvet. "Empty," he said. He dropped the lid and moved the box to the top of the safe.

"Why would he keep an empty box?"

Kade shrugged. "Beats me. Out here, some people buy so many they lose track of what they've got. Maybe he lent them out."

"Pretty sure I'd never forget whether I owned a gun or not. Let alone let someone else use it."

"He's the type who would buy a new shirt so he wouldn't have to do laundry. You remember how he does business."

Elizabeth did. She'd been caught up in Guy's shady dealings before. His employee took the blame, but there was little doubt in her mind that Guy was far from innocent. "I can't imagine having more of anything than I know what to do with."

"People like Guy don't think about that. They don't consider how their carelessness affects anyone. Everything is disposable. Including people. Like George." Kade trailed off.

Elizabeth was quiet, thinking. The memory continued to tug at the back of her mind until her eyes went wide with recognition. "I'll be right back. I need some air—"

Her mind whirling, she bolted for the door. Hands numb, she reached for the knob. Her body was all motion, a singular realization driving her movement.

She heard Kade call out behind her. "But you'll get soaked!"

Elizabeth didn't stop to respond. She'd already dialed the sheriff.

36

DESSERTS COVERED THE KITCHEN island. Silky pumpkin whipped with eggs had settled into a flakey crust topped with curls of chocolate. Brownies swirled with pumpkin and chocolate had nuts in some of the squares, none in others. A six-tier cake was missing a slice. Elizabeth would have bet money that it was cloaked in thick, cream cheese icing.

The air in the Blau household was perfumed with cinnamon, cardamon, and nutmeg. Casey had taken seasonal baked goods to a whole new level, and Elizabeth fought the urge to gorge on the spread.

Jo arrived, and Elizabeth gave her a fair warning. "As you can see, we are planning death by sugar for the guests."

Casey removed a sheet of pumpkin Graham crackers from the oven. Two slid off the corner and tumbled to the floor. Crumbs littered the tile. Leia snapped one up before Casey banished her from the kitchen.

Rhett, seated in his booster, smeared the better half of a pumpkin muffin onto his face.

"I can see that," Jo said.

With a broom and dust pan, Casey swept up the bulk of the spilled crackers. "These will cool, then we can taste-test the s'mores."

"S'mores?"

Elizabeth put one hand over her stomach and puffed out her cheeks. "Two words: bourbon marshmallows." Elizabeth took the dust pan from Casey and tipped the contents into the trash while he washed his hands.

"I'm determined," Casey said, drying his hands on a towel.

Jo nodded. "Okay, I see the level we've reached here. Liz, any chance we could go for a quick walk?"

"I could use a break from the sugar," Elizabeth said. "It's making me lightheaded."

"Sure, sure. Go. I'll be here, making my eighth batch of caramel." Casey lifted a marshmallow from a plastic container and set it on a warm cracker. With powdered sugar-dusted hands, he scratched his forehead with the side of his arm. "Hey, Liz, while you're out there, could you check on the girls?"

"Got it," Elizabeth said. She lifted a thick flannel from the coatrack and draped it around her shoulders.

Outside, a cold wind bit at their cheeks, freed strands of hair from under their beanie hats. They skip-walked into the barn, eager to get out of the elements.

Inside the warm barn, Elizabeth yanked on the heavy door to slide it closed. She faced Jo, anticipating. "Out with it."

"We can't use the shelter."

"What?"

Jo slid her hands into her pockets and shrugged. "Corbin has an inspector coming the next day. Throwing a party the night before doesn't work."

"So, we change the date."

Jo shook her head. "No can do. We've got invites out and a zillion other commitments already set."

"Okay. So, we need a new location. It's not a big deal." Elizabeth paced in front of a stall, thinking aloud. "Nope. It's a huge deal. Where can we find a place for two hundred guests, the band, and the food to feed them all? It's too soon!"

"About that. There's more."

Elizabeth groaned. Two nearby goats bleated in response. She reached for the bucket of treats and dished out an offering to the nannies. "I'm listening, but I'm already unhappy about it."

"We've only had six people sign up to bring chili."

"That's not going to work."

"And—"

"And?"

"The Checkered Bandanas broke up."

Elizabeth frowned. "Who?"

"The band. From Kaycee? They got into a huge fight on a round-up. I'm told the bassist is no longer speaking to the lead vocalist."

Elizabeth rubbed her temples to quell the tension building underneath her skin. "This is a disaster. An unprecedented mess. What are we going to do? We have to cancel. That's all we can do. Tell Corbin we can try again next year. Put out a message."

"You think we should quit."

She sat on a hay bale and put her head into her hands. "I wanted this to work, Jo. I wanted it." Elizabeth tasted the falseness in her words, then willed them to be true. "I need to stop wanting things. That's what it is. Every time I want something to fit, to line up and work out, it doesn't. It's high time I dash my hopes."

Jo put her hands on her hips and cocked an eyebrow. "Done with the pity party yet?"

Elizabeth sniffed and wiped off a tear with her fist. She thought of her situation with Kade, his uncle. The job she didn't love. Her waffling over where to live and when. Her son's speech delay. The desire to give him his very own barn full of animals but instead settling for a plastic farm set. "Ever have those seasons when you get knocked down no matter what you do?"

"We all do. But if there is one thing I know about you, it's that you didn't come all the way out here to fail. The Elizabeth I know didn't go through fire just to crumple like a used tissue when things get hard. Where's the brave friend of mine?"

Jo's kindness washed over Elizabeth like a warm hug. She took a deep breath. Her friend was right. Yes, the circumstances stank. This was an impossible situation for which there was no likely solution.

But dang it, she was going to do her best to find one.

"What you're saying is that we've got some phone calls to make."

Fall down seven, stand up eight.

37

A N HOUR LATER, JO left them each with a to-do list and a Plan B for pulling off the event. They'd chosen a farm theme: blue gingham, straw, warm candles, and other autumnal tones.

Elizabeth's list included calling every event venue in the county.

"Shouldn't take too long. There aren't many to choose from." Jo shrugged into her coat, then swung a scarf around her neck.

"What do I do if they're taken?"

Jo slung her purse over her shoulder. "Pray they aren't. Call some musicians, too? Thanks."

After Jo left, Casey dragged out his recipe books, cards, and scribblings. He spread them over the countertop.

Elizabeth wrote Places in her notebook, then paused, her pencil above the paper. How did she, the newest resident of the planning crew, get stuck with locations? She tapped the eraser end of the pencil against the paper, willing a solution to present itself.

Instead, her phone rang. *Kade.* She scrambled to answer it.

"Hi," she said, and attempted to squelch any desperation from her voice. "Long time no talk."

"George was arrested."

A muscle on Elizabeth's eyelid twitched, and she bit her lip. "What? When? Why?" A wave of guilt sent chills down her spine. Her parrot-like responses betrayed her inability to process what he said.

"They found a gun in his house. It had his prints on it, and it had been fired recently."

"Kade. I'm so sorry," she said. She stumbled on the words, spitting them out like watermelon seeds. They were half-truths, bitter and slimy. A knot caught in her throat as she considered the implications. "Maybe it's a coincidence. It might not have anything to do with Guy."

Kade was silent. Through the speaker came garbled conversation in the background. Was he at the shop?

"How do you know it has something to do with Guy?"

Elizabeth blanched. She had stepped into a pile of yuck, knee deep. "I...uh...didn't...I hadn't..." But she did. She had.

Kade interrupted her. "It's all over the news which means it's on the lips of every gossip around. How could he have been so sloppy? I bet someone saw it at the Open House. Waited to say anything until it would knock him down. If Guy wasn't...gone, I would have blamed him for it."

Elizabeth battled nausea. Kade didn't know what she'd done. Yet. "I'm so sorry to hear that."

"Are you? George said you hadn't been by as much. Asked if you were okay. I was wondering if you'd turned on him, too."

"Of course not, it's just that I—" But Elizabeth couldn't share what she'd seen the day she met George. Couldn't bear to out herself. She had to wait for the investigation to conclude. Shame ate at her heartstrings.

"I shouldn't have called," Kade said. "I'm not in my right mind. Ever been in a place where you're convinced there's a target on your back? Like life keeps piling it on because once you've been knocked down, what's a few more blows?"

Elizabeth's gut ached. She mumbled an evasive reply, but Kade cut her off.

"I'll catch up later, okay?"

Then the line went dead.

38

ELIZABETH EASED OFF THE two-lane highway into a wide, oval yard next to a long, white building. Gray shingles and a wide front porch made for a welcoming entrance. Stubby, dry grass whipped into brief patches lined by taller sedges at the periphery. There wasn't room for two hundred cars here, but she'd cross each hurdle as they came.

The first was to verify that the inside wasn't full of cobwebs and had the promised dance floor.

At the front door, she found a pine log stretched between two tall posts, likely from the same tree. U-shaped prints in the dust indicated a hitching post with good use. Near the far end of the building sat a large shed, its doors barred and secured with a padlock.

Jo's SUV joined Elizabeth's car, a sedan behind it. A woman with a unibrow and two thick braids rolled out of the maroon four-door, a ring of keys in hand.

"Vicki. Vicki Crane. I run the Hall's social media and reservations. Not the programming though. Well, I do the paint and sip nights, but I'm running out of wall space. Might need to come up with something else."

Elizabeth held out her hand. "Call me Liz," she said. "I'd introduce myself, but seeing as how we were in the same scout troop, it feels silly," Jo said.

The woman smiled. "Right, I'll show you the hall. Give you a tour. I know you've been here a time or two, Jo, but your friend might get into the history."

Elizabeth took an instant liking to Vicki. She reminded Elizabeth of a chicken, all urgent business and blustery movements.

"I'll make myself scarce for that part," Jo said.

"Take all the time you need. Get out your little tape measures and what have you. We take five hundred down—"

"Zeb said we'd get a discount, since we're a non-profit," Jo said. She followed Vicki up the steps to the doors.

Elizabeth joined the women, her footsteps creaking on the pine board porch.

"History first, business after." Vicki held the door for them. "Now, where was I? Ah. Kearney Hall was built in the fifties by a group of neighbors who wanted somewhere to gather. We started the foundation over a decade ago to bring back some of the events from our past. Give something back to the community."

"Very cool," Elizabeth said. "I love open space."

They'd entered the main area of the hall. The long room opened up with lots of potential for seating. A huge hearth mirrored the front doors. Pictures lined the hall.

Vicki stopped at a picture of a group of people on the porch outside. "With a little seed money from local businesses, we made the first major repairs and were able to reopen. A few years of dances, weddings, and meetings, and we've been able to keep a roof on the place. Next up is getting the old fireplace modernized. New chimney, the works."

Vicki moved off toward the fireplace, chattering with Jo. Elizabeth paused to peer at the old photograph. In it, a large group of people crowded the steps out front, all in western attire. The photograph had a slight blur, as though it had been taken in motion.

Elizabeth squinted at the people in the frame.

"Jo—is that..."

Jo was across the room, chatting with Vicki. Elizabeth peered at the faces in front of her. There, Guy and George smiled into the camera. Dressed in outdoor gear, they would have fit into any hunting catalog. Flannel shirts, cargo pants, worn boots, and caps complete with ear flaps turned them into mountain men. Brothers. The so-called tech experts looked like they'd pay to avoid a computer if they could help it.

Closer inspection revealed a familiar, silver-haired woman at the side of the picture. She squatted to pat a chocolate lab seated at her feet. Elizabeth was certain this was a younger version of Laney Horowitz.

Most of the other faces were unrecognizable to Elizabeth—except one.

She'd missed him on the first pass. In washed out jeans, a dark flannel, and dusty boots, he was the opposite of a pristine businessman from the big city. Decades younger, he had a carefree grin, as though he'd spent the day playing cowboy on the range.

Ira, the investor she'd met at the brewery, leaned over the hitching post in the picture. With a smile worth capturing, he gazed straight into the camera.

"I figured you'd spot a familiar face or two."

"I do. Small towns and all."

Vicki joined them by the wall. "What do you think of the space?"

Elizabeth had been so focused on the picture she'd missed the rest of the tour.

Jo nudged Elizabeth with her elbow. "Can you picture yourself out there on the dance floor? I keep meaning to ask if you're bringing a date."

Elizabeth appraised the wooden dance floor. "Not sure if he's coming," she said. When Jo raised her eyebrows, Elizabeth filled her in on the conversation from the day before.

"Clint said as much. You know, Laney always said George was the only one worth working for. He was loud, but you always knew what he was thinking. Said the others were sneaky. It's a shame if it turns out he changed."

Elizabeth turned back to the picture on the wall and regarded the younger versions of people she'd met. Considered who they were back then, who they became. *Do we all shift so much over a lifetime?*

"I'm worried Kade is one who changed."

"Despite what some men claim, it does happen."

39

ELIZABETH SLIPPED THE RING on and off her own finger for the whole drive to the sheriff's department. It had become a fidget for her, something she did without thinking.

Married. Not married. Married. *Gone.*

When no one called her, she planned to bring it in. Then one disruption after another kept her from dropping by. It wasn't like you could make lost-and-found appointments.

Today, it would happen. It couldn't wait a moment longer.

The sheriffs had their offices in a shared lot with the city police. The tidy, tan, modern buildings were far from the adorable vintage brick shops of Main Street and blocks away from Kade's.

Clint's office was never on her way to anything.

"Good morning," Elizabeth sang as she pushed the glass door across the cheap, industrial carpet. The sheriff's department smelled like old coffee, cleaning fluids, and something human she couldn't name. The front area was far from welcoming. There was a vinyl couch, a low table littered with old magazines, and a water cooler. The reception desk was its own enclosure with a roll down barrier, should it be needed. The woman behind the desk pressed her lips together at the sight of her newest interruption.

"Hello, Ms. Blau. Let me guess. You have clues for a dead-end case? No, wait. Someone is stalking you. Or you got a cat, and you need help getting him out of a tree."

Elizabeth did her best not to roll her eyes. "It's so good to see you, too."

"A social call, then? Whichever it is, Sheriff Wolf isn't available, and no you may not barge in on his office."

More than once in the year she'd lived in Sheridan County, Elizabeth had steamrolled her way into these offices, whether to demand Clint get moving on an investigation or because she'd been called in for questioning. His employee had never liked Elizabeth, but there seemed to be little she could do to change that.

"Don't have a cat...yet. Actually, I'm here to see you."

"Oh goodie," the woman said. Sarcasm dripped from her words. "To what do I owe the pleasure?" She tapped her turquoise-painted nails on the counter. Behind her, a shelf was lined with pictures of her dachshunds. A giant water bottle anchored her desktop, and she had a knitting project rolled up and set aside.

Elizabeth withdrew the ring and held it out. "I found this on the South Piney Trail. I put my number on the chalkboard, but no one called. Figured I should turn it in as it looks real to me."

Wolf's secretary reached for the ring with her claws. Her sky-blue nails shone as the woman held the ring up to her desk lamp. Elizabeth noted her mauve lipstick feathered around the edges. A dozen blue pens in a mug that said *Coffee Saves Lives* rested at the woman's elbow.

"Someone is in the doghouse for losing this." She slid it back to Elizabeth along with a form. "Fill this out, including specific details about the ring. If no one claims it in sixty days, it's yours. We only have so much room. You wouldn't believe the things people lose. Bring it back up when you finish, and I'll give you a copy."

Elizabeth retreated to the lumpy, vinyl couch and low coffee table with the ring, form, and a cheap ballpoint pen from the cup on the counter.

The first few questions were her contact information, then the where and when of the find. At the space for describing the item, Elizabeth listed the ring as gold with a diamond. She squinted at the inside to verify the engravings once more.

Sheriff Wolf entered from a back door, file folder in hand. He stopped at the sight of Elizabeth.

"Ms. Blau," he said. "Don't tell me something else has happened. We've had a fender bender, a domestic, and a fraud complaint come in, and it's not even noon."

Elizabeth held up the ring. "Turning in something I found, then I'll be out of your hair."

"As you were, then." Wolf nodded, then handed his secretary a file. The folder was marked *To be signed*, and one of the signature blue pens was clipped to the front.

Elizabeth returned to her task. In the description box, she scribbled down the date, then triple checked the initials.

"M. A. R.," Elizabeth wrote, then stopped. "Wait." Her breath caught in her throat as she reread the date and then ran through the math. Twice. "Uh, Sheriff?"

Wolf and his secretary paused their discussion, the first with curiosity, the second with irritation.

Elizabeth approached them with the ring and her paper. She held the ring out to Clint. "This was Laney's."

"What?" He blinked several times, like a startled parrot. "Laney Horowitz?"

Elizabeth nodded. "I'm not one hundred percent sure. I mean, I didn't see her wear it or anything. But she was on that trail the day I found it. There's a date on there. Could be her anniversary, which of course you could verify. Those are her initials though, because the M—"

"Is for Melanie," Clint finished, staring at the ring. "When did you find it?" He reached in his pocket to withdraw a small, zip-locked plastic bag.

"On our way back down. Jo and I, that day Laney—died. We saw her on our way up, when she was on her way home."

Clint held out the open bag, and Elizabeth dropped the ring inside. He sealed it, frowning at the contents. "Wallace will be glad to get it back, if it is hers. Heartbroken, too. I'll take a look at that form, if you don't mind."

"But I didn't find it near her," Elizabeth said. "Or...uh, near where you found her." He'd said they found Laney by the water. While parts of the mountainside trail lined the creek, at others, the path was sided by a buffer of bushes and trees. "It was on the trail. I could show you, of course."

Clint weighed the ring in his hand, thinking. "Could mean something, could mean nothing. Either way, we'll get this logged. I'll call Wallace and see if we have a match."

Head down, thumbs tapping, she ran straight into George.

"I'm so sorry," Elizabeth said. "I was doing that thing other people do that I can't stand. Walkers have a lower risk of injury than runners, but I assume that's only if they look where they're going."

"S'alright," he said, a stiff response. He carried a large, clear bag in which she spotted a wallet and keys.

"Oh," Elizabeth said. His obvious release, the return of his belongings, an unspoken reality between them. "Um—can I give you a ride home?" Guilt and confusion raced through her bloodstream. She offered a bandage.

He regarded her. A range of emotions flashed across his face. Anger, sadness, and uncertainty. He settled on resigned. "Are you sure you want to be seen with a criminal like me?"

"Of course," she said. "I owe you."

"I don't want your pity. I don't want anyone's pity."

The man from the open house had returned, bristling and bitter. She couldn't blame him.

"I'm hoping you still want my friendship."

40

ELIZABETH HAD A BASKET of gingham tablecloths in the back of her car. She could have picnicked for days.

Jo had called in a favor to the Parkdale quilting group, and they'd dug through their stores. Along with their neighbors in Dayton and Ranchester, the members found every scrap of checkered fabric in the tri-town area. The result of that treasure hunt, the yards of fabric, spools of thread, and everything between, lay folded and ready for the event.

There would be some hemming, Jo said. Some piecing, too. But table covers were done. Elizabeth was grateful—and late.

Her phone's GPS directed her south toward what she hoped was I-90. Time was short, and she had a nagging to-do list. Hours from the event and Elizabeth was doing her best to avoid panic.

When a black streak zipped in front of the car, Elizabeth slammed on her brakes. Her hatchback fishtailed before skidding to a halt. Breath heaving, she was half on the road, half into the soft, crumbled shale shoulder.

Elizabeth popped open her door and stumbled out, shaken.

On the side of the road, a standard poodle watched her. Its tongue lolled. Elizabeth watched as her nerves settled. She reached for a spare leash from inside her car and considered her opponent.

The dog panted as she approached. "Hey there, furball," she said, pitching her voice to a saccharine tone. "You almost killed me back there. You okay? I'm nice. Are you nice?"

She stepped closer. The dog took a tentative sniff in her general direction. When he—it was a he, she verified—stepped toward her, tail wagging, she ventured a pat. "Where are your people?"

Elizabeth looked up the road. A trim, white farmhouse with green shutters sat in front of the prairie backdrop. It nestled at a small crossroads sided by a deep creek with a bank of cottonwoods lining its boundaries. With a quick snatch of the dog's collar, she was off to see who was home.

A tiny, older woman answered. "I don't let tourists use the bathroom," she said before her face appeared in the crack. "They leave it a mess. I mean not you, you look normal. But you let one in, you have to let them all, you know."

Elizabeth pressed at the door before the woman could shut it. "I'm here because I found this dog." She gave a quick tug on the leash. The poodle bounded up the steps in greeting. He muscled his face into the gap at the door, tail wagging.

"Oooh! You found Jack." She opened the door wide, and the dog sniffed the expanse of her denim apron. "That Houdini has broken out twice this week. The owners have tried every lock available. Somehow, he continues to bust free. Poor things have only had him a handful of days. Bouncy dogs take some getting used to. He does love my cooking, their Jack—"

"Would you be able to call them? The owners. Or at least take care of him until they can get back here? I'm in a bit of a hurry."

"Of course. Jack and I go way back to Sunday night. Don't we, boy?"

Elizabeth held tight to Jack's collar while she unhooked the leash. "Are the owners home? If it's close, I could take him."

"My guess is they are at work, but I've got their number." As Jack bounded into the house, she continued. "Poor things, trying to sell their land. Getting ready to pick up and move and go and get a dog. Some people don't have sense to shake a stick at. Nice folks, though."

"Do they have a gate? I could always drop him off."

The woman shook her head. Buttery, silver ringlets framed her soft and wrinkled face. "No, more of the outdoorsy type. What's that called? Oh, yeah, glampers. They tired of being off-grid, something about having too much space. Whatever that is. City folk are a different lot. Anywho, so long as no one builds a cookie cutter neighborhood here, I figure it should be okay, right?"

"I suppose so," Elizabeth said. She'd become so twisted into the woman's narrative she'd almost forgotten her purpose.

"I know why the caged bird sings..." the woman trailed off. "When natural-born adventurers are restrained, they find a way out. It's a question of when, not if. Jack is no exception. You hurry along now, dear. Jack and I will whip up a batch of doggie biscuits, eh, boy?"

"Thank you. You live in a beautiful spot," Elizabeth said. "I'm not surprised Jack wants to explore."

The woman stroked the dog's soft fur. "He's a nice boy. Sometimes the universe is cruel to the brave."

"I hear that," Liz said, stroking the dog's soft ears. "But Jack, stay out of the road next time. You'll get yourself flattened."

"True," the woman said. "But if we didn't have an end date, where would we find our motivation?"

41

KEARNEY HALL GLOWED FROM the lights strung inside and out. At the front door, the decorations committee—Jo and Hannah Black, giving Elizabeth an excuse to bow out—had stacked hay bales, pumpkins, and corn stalks. Inside, they'd strung garlands of autumnal leaves. Cheery checked tablecloths were topped with their thrifted vases bursting with sunflowers. A crackling fire welcomed guests, beckoning them toward the small stage in the corner. Mic stands and amps waited for the music. Elizabeth turned a small circle, observing the effect. They'd done it. The hall was beautiful.

For her part, Elizabeth had transformed a small counter off the kitchen into a beverage station. She'd topped a golden table runner with a picture of Rhett and Leia posing with a pumpkin and tacked a menu of offerings to the wall.

Activities were off to a busy start. For the trick-a-thon, pet owners had the opportunity to show off their top dog tricks. There was the lab who could balance several stacked cups on his nose. A pug-Chihuahua who could dance to hip hop, and a husky who could howl in time with a Rihanna song.

Corbin was in his element as the evening's emcee. He welcomed guests, directed attendees to the silent auction tables, and chatted with the crowd. He perched on a high stool parked at the corner of the short stage. The event was a sold-out success, and his grin stretched across the room.

At her makeshift bar, Elizabeth held court. Foam ran over her hand. She'd overfilled a pint glass, though the bulk of the golden ale settled within. She reached for a rag to wipe up the spill and passed the drink to the eager attendee.

The man, bedecked in a chambray shirt, knotted kerchief, and starched blue jeans, accepted the glass with a hearty, "Cheers!" He chugged half the contents, then smacked his lips. "Per-fection," he said, before lifting his glass in tribute and moving off into the crowd.

"Tastes better than that Colorado swill," Big Ricky said as the stranger moved off. "Come on, Blau. Time to let ol' Gibson retire and let you take over. When will we see you behind a real bar?"

"One day, my prayers will be answered, Rick. Until then, I've got to be patient."

Ricky leaned one elbow on the countertop and scanned the room. "You know, I had a wife. Once. She left me." He took a sip of his beer but kept his eyes averted. "I prayed every day for fate to turn my way. Sat in that old house and waited."

He looked at her, and for the first time, Elizabeth considered the depth within the man. Deep crows' feet framed eyes the color of a worn saddle. He wandered a land of nostalgia she couldn't understand. She saw pain, though. And pleading. "Prayers are one thing. Doing the good work alongside them, that's the real ticket. Wait if you must, but don't miss your chances." Ricky offered her a silent toast and moved on to watch the show.

Elizabeth was silent. Ricky's words sank into her heart, challenging her.

42

ELIZABETH WAS UNDER THE spell of Ricky's words.

"Ma'am, that's going to—"

The warning landed a moment too late in Elizabeth's brain. Again the soft bubbles spilled over her knuckles.

"Dang it, I keep doing that. So sorry," she said to the man. She wiped at the cup and handed it over to him. "We brewed this with local pumpkins."

The IPA was a massive hit. She'd directed all orders to Buzz who promised to have the beer on tap next week. It stung to funnel sales through another person, as gracious as Buzz was with sharing his facility. Elizabeth thought of Ricky's words.

"I thought the goal was to put the beer in the glass," Casey said, a wry smile on his face. He and Danny stepped up to her counter for a drink.

Danny had a keg of his own wild ale kicked up on a blue hand truck. He and Elizabeth maneuvered it into the ice and attached the tap.

Casey continued to tease. "Maybe I've been doing it wrong this whole time. Sure is warm in here."

Elizabeth pointed the keg hose his way in a mock threat. "What did you say about needing to cool off?"

"Hold up," Danny said, as he shifted his set-up, careful not to crush his toes. "Don't waste a good beer on this guy. Or at least, save me a glass first."

Elizabeth liked Daniel Sorensen. Another home brewer, they'd traded tips, tricks, and recipes in the months since she'd met him at a local contest. His brews were unique, crafted from wild yeasts and brewed in hollowed-out logs.

"Hey," Danny said. "For what it's worth, I'm not taking him up on the offer."

"Which offer?"

"Ira's. He told me you were in the ring, too. I decided it's not for me. I'm more of a lone wolf, not a collaborator. I don't think I'd be able to handle a corporate overlord—however deep his pockets may be. And...he told me y'all were in talks, too," Danny said. He held her gaze. "I didn't want that between us."

A flush crept across Elizabeth's cheeks. "Yeah, uh. No worries. I mean, it wouldn't have been a problem. Either way."

Elizabeth scrambled to find sincerity in her words. She continued to trip over Danny's news. The idea that Ira was shopping competition unnerved her. Was it a competition? She needed to talk to the investor, get the story straight.

"Casey?" Elizabeth tapped her brother on the shoulder. He'd had his eyes and ears trained on the band, tapping his foot in time to the music. "Take over for a minute, will you?"

"Oh no," her brother said, "I know how this goes. You ditch me, and I'm stuck pretending like I know how to make this stuff when people ask questions."

"Come on, please?"

Casey held out his hands in front of his chest. "No way. I haven't been able to place any bids yet. There's a ski weekend with my name on it. Well, not yet, I need to put my name on it."

Danny scooted past Casey. "I'll take a turn at the taps. Go for it."

"Thank you, Danny," Elizabeth said. "So glad some people were raised right."

"We grew up in the same house," Casey called behind her.

It was standing room only as Elizabeth wove her way through the crowd toward the door. She would call Ira and take the offer. She wouldn't lose this chance.

Elizabeth was so focused she walked right into Kade's arms. He caught her, then held her away from him. "Whoa, where's the fire?"

"Sorry. So sorry. I was on my way outside and—"

"Would you like to dance?" Kade gave her shoulders a squeeze as he watched her expression.

"Huh?"

"I thought we could talk. You know, while I spin you around the dance floor. I've been thinking a lot. About the future."

He dropped his hands to hers and lifted one a little and off to the side. He stepped to one side and then back, a slow two-step. Elizabeth followed, unsure of her footing.

"I'm sorry for the last few weeks. I had a lot to work out, then with George...I was a jerk. I got twisted back up into my family's past, and I got distracted. From us. I won't let that happen again."

Kade smiled at her, hope in his expression, and she knew she couldn't wait any longer. Before she could second-guess her decision, she dove into sharing. "Seventy percent of relationships end in their first year."

"What?" Kade's face crumpled. His cheeks puckered and he blinked. "Where did that come from?"

"I'm not ready to move in together. Not yet. I've got things I want to do first."

He flinched, as though she'd thrown each word at him, an assault. "I don't understand. I thought we were good. Better than good."

"I need to prove I can." Saying the words out loud made her confidence waver, as though she'd found the selfish edge. "I need...a little more time, that's all."

Kade dropped his hands from where he'd held her, stepped back into the crowd, and let it envelope him.

Oh, Liz, she thought. *What have you done?*

43

E LIZABETH SECOND GUESSED EVERY word she'd said for the next five minutes. Jo found her pacing by the front door.

"I'm an idiot," she told Jo. "First class."

"Maybe. But to be honest, that's a low bar. Sergeant Idiot would take a lot more effort on your part."

"Why did I say anything? It's not like he asked me to move in with him. He asked me to dance. I was so wound up by the thought of competition for the deal, I blew right past him."

They ducked into the kitchen where the food trays refilled as fast as the volunteers could make it happen. The quarters were tight, but Jo ran an assembly line. Elizabeth recognized a few of the faces from Laney's memorial at the Women's Club.

Jo sliced into another pie from a stack on the counter. She parceled the wedges out onto compostable plates. "The man has been through a lot—"

"I knew it." Elizabeth threw up her hands. "I am the worst."

"—I was going to say, and so have you. It makes sense that sometimes your motives won't align. Both of your lives are full, complicated. That's life, Liz. That's relationships. All that talk about fifty-fifty nonsense is magazine editors trying to get sales. In reality, you're often trading the heavy load back and forth. Right now, neither of you is free to hold it, and that's what's causing the hiccups."

"What if I never want to hold the load? I feel like I held so much of it with Nick that I...Maybe I'm broken, Jo. What if I can't help carry anyone else's baggage? Like I'm worn down, too weak to handle it."

Elizabeth flattened herself against the fridge as a volunteer brought a case of wine into the galley kitchen for uncorking. Jo handed pie slices to the crowd. When one disappeared, she sliced into another.

Jo plated eight slices, doling out the last of that pie. "Then you'll miss out on a great guy, and I, as your friend, am going to save a giant 'I told you so' for when you finally realize it."

Elizabeth closed her eyes and sank farther against the fridge. The hum of the surrounding helpers was a welcome din. She knew she should help, get back to her service bar, but she wallowed in self-pity instead, pinned by her doubts.

"Am I always doomed to work for some man? Have my future offered on conditions determined by a guy in my life?"

Jo tilted her chin toward the great room. Clint had Rhett in his arms. The off-duty sheriff did a shuffle-step in time to the music, watching the gleeful face of the little boy he held. Rhett had a grin plastered from ear to ear. He clapped his hands a few times to the beat.

"Tell me," Jo said. "Is that such a bad thing?"

Elizabeth watched her son, her favorite person, her world, dance to the fiddle tune.

"Okay, I may have promoted myself to Corporal Idiot."

"Ms. Blau." Clint held up Rhett's hand to wave it in her direction. He always used a formal address when he had to talk business. "Can I borrow you for a minute? I saw Mr. Horowitz."

44

J O WAS HAPPY TO plunk Rhett in a chair with a piece of chocolate pie.

"I've got this under control," she said. "Take too long, and I'll give him a second slice," she added with a wink.

Elizabeth followed Wolf out to the wrap-around porch. He moved toward the western corner of the covered space and leaned over the railing.

Along the porch there were two benches hewn from sizable logs and an outdoor chandelier piled high with antlers. Stacked bales of hay blocked the highway view and turned attention toward the west and the oncoming sunset.

On the edge of the parking area, a small pack of dogs raced and played. With some moveable fencing and a few willing volunteers, Jo had created a space for well-behaved pups to romp and wrestle. "Can't have an animal rescue benefit that doesn't welcome some type of animal," she'd explained.

Elizabeth watched a pair of water spaniels tug on the same toy while the sheriff consulted a document on his phone. He held the bright screen away from his face and then inched it closer, squinting. "It's about time I get new readers," he said. "Jo caught me taking a picture of the mail and then enlarging the image so I could read it better." Wolf made a reverse pinching gesture with two of his fingers.

"You said you'd talked to Wallace?" Elizabeth bit her lip. Interruptions came faster than she could escape them. What if someone signed with Ira in the next few minutes? She'd spend a lifetime kicking herself.

"I did. He said thank you, by the way. Wanted you to know most people would've kept it. I'd have to agree."

"Actually, Michigan researchers found the higher the value, the more likely someone will turn it in."

"He was grateful."

Elizabeth eyed the parking lot. It was full. Cars stretched along the side of the hallway. A garbled voice from inside the building announced the imminent auction through the speakers around the dance floor. She had minutes before someone would notice her absence. Elizabeth had signed up to be a runner for the auction items, and Jo would send a posse for her if she didn't show soon. She glanced at her watch. "Thanks for letting me know. If there's nothing else—"

She started for the door, but Wolf reached for her sleeve. "Wait, Ms. Blau. There's one more thing."

Elizabeth faced Wolf. He held his phone out to her. On its screen was the image of an older man and woman, his arm over her shoulders, she holding a handful of sunflowers. They smiled at the camera, the late afternoon sun in their silvery hair.

"Look closer," Wolf said, and handed her the phone. "You may be due for glasses, too. Sneaks up on a body."

Frowning at his gibe, Elizabeth accepted the phone. She peered at the couple. Scrutinized their posture, their clothing, the way the clouds darkened behind them.

Then she saw it.

"It's around her neck."

Wolf nodded.

Laney wore a slim gold necklace in the photo. The ring Elizabeth found was the pendant. She had her left hand over Wallace's right. Her hand was ring-free.

"So, what happened to the chain?"

Wolf pressed back from the railing. "I hope to have that answer within the hour. Ryland is out there now, but we don't have long before it's dark."

"It could be in dirt, or lying in the creek..."

"You see why I have more questions than answers."

"What if he doesn't find it? How can you be sure he's looking in the right place?"

"As my grandpa always said, a burden shared is a burden halved." Wolf tipped his hat toward her. "If you'll excuse me, I'm going to distract myself from the wait by bidding an exorbitant amount on a sewing table I know Jo is after."

Elizabeth brushed her fingers across her own clavicle, thinking. She reached for her phone to call Ira, only to realize his number was in her purse inside the hall.

"Liz," Jo called out the door. "We've got an auction to run!"

45

"WHEN THE AUCTIONEER SAYS sold, bring the item to the back table. You'll hand it to the cashier."

Jo whispered instructions in Elizabeth's ear as they entered the hall. Corbin was mid-speech at the microphone. At the back of the hall, a handful of people fussed over a pair of cash boxes and a credit card machine.

"Run the item from one table to the other table. Can do." Elizabeth wondered if she could sneak in a call between items. Maybe a quick text that read *Regarding your business proposal, I'm in.* She whipped out her phone.

"Auctions go fast. The cashiers will keep a rough total of what we bring in. I'll share that with the crowd—unless you want to—then ask for last-minute donations. Then we ask them to skedaddle, but in a nice way. They go home, and we clean until it looks cleaner than when they built it. Got it?"

Elizabeth had been staring back at the photos on the wall. "Hmm? Oh, yes. Golf weekends, paintings, and bottles of wine to the back. Then ask for more cash before kicking everyone out." She could see the one from the remodel from where she stood. Two of those who'd helped were gone. She saw Laney's face, the faith that she would make a difference evident in her smile.

And she had. She'd helped Kade's mom. The woman had provided for Kade throughout his life. She'd defied her boss to make it happen, too. Taken company money to do what Guy should have done from the beginning.

But it wasn't just Guy, Elizabeth thought.

"Jo?"

"Hmm?" Jo held a list in one hand and checked items off it with a pen held in the other.

"What was Laney's job before she retired?"

"She was their accountant by the time she left. Started as a basic bookkeeper. Why do you ask?"

A screech of the microphone interrupted Elizabeth's reply.

"Okay, y'all. We've got one more song from our band before the auction starts." Corbin stepped down from the stage, and the band tucked back into a song.

Elizabeth didn't hear Jo. As the fiddle player drew a bow across the strings to check his tuning, a familiar face mounted the single step to the stage.

The band leader leaned toward the microphone. He brushed his hair out of his eyes and spoke into the mouthpiece.

"Thank you all. We'll be taking a dinner break, but you'll have a chance to bid on some amazing items during the auction. It's all for a noble cause, and we are so happy to be here celebrating with you. For this last song, though, we've brought up a friend of ours to join us, George Henderson."

George doffed his hat to the crowd and took a seat. The band's leader continued. "I think you'll all agree that he's a mighty fine picker. He chose this song for us tonight, an old favorite."

Elizabeth stared at the stage. She watched as George nodded at the fiddle player and they were off. Fingers flew across frets as those on stage gave the tune their all. Elizabeth tapped in time to the music, as though her foot had a life of its own. The crowd clapped in time, cheering louder as the pace quickened.

The fiddle player signaled the end of the song with a long draw, his head bowed over his instrument. As the crowd erupted into applause, she watched George wipe his forehead with the back of his hand. The bandmates took turns shaking his hand before they all ambled off the stage and faded into the crowd.

"My mom always loved that song," Kade said over her shoulder.

Elizabeth's emotions swirled inside her like a dust storm. Unseen turbulence made for an imbalance, a sense of change on the horizon.

George's playing was beautiful, effortless. Yet she knew what it cost him to put himself out there, exposed.

Out there. Exposed. Like a photograph.

"He's been here the whole time, I can't believe it," Elizabeth said.

"What? Who?"

"There were four of them, together. Laney, too. I have to find Clint," Elizabeth said. She clutched at Kade's jacket. "Will you help me find him?"

Kade searched her eyes, his brows crinkled. "Of course. He's around here somewhere. But maybe we should get dessert first. I bet Jo would let us sneak a slice and take it out—"

Elizabeth shook her head. "No, no time. Please. I mean, thank you, but no. I need to find Clint. He needs to see the picture of the founders. You go that way." She pointed toward the north end of the building where a small side door brought in fresh air to the stuffy hall. Despite an outdoor temperature dip in sync with the sunset, inside the room was warm. People spilled out into the night, chatting as they leaned against the side of the building. "I'll go out front. He can't be far."

"Are you sure we need to find him now?"

"We have to, before it gets dark!"

46

BEFORE KADE COULD PRESS her for information, Elizabeth was off.

Guests packed every nook and cranny of the hall. The space was a sea of denim and boots, gingham and hats.

And the turnout had been impressive.

She stopped at each table, questioned every clump of guests as to whether they'd seen the sheriff. She asked neighbors and her co-workers. Corbin and Hannah. Big Ricky and his buddies. People watching their kids. Members of the band.

Sheriff Wolf was nowhere to be found.

Elizabeth retreated to a wall to scan again. She'd worked up a sweat looking for the man. She whispered under her breath, "Come on, Clint, where *are* you?"

Behind her, the auctioneer claimed the microphone. "You'll want to have your bandanas up. Wave 'em high so I can see them."

Dozens in the crowd waved numbered bandanas, Jo's idea. They'd spent an afternoon gluing the fabric to fan backs to make for easy waving. Elizabeth had to admit, they came out great.

"If you are the highest bidder, you'll want to make your way down to the back of the room. Our runners will meet you there where we have a host of volunteers ready to collect your generous donations."

Elizabeth bit her lip, then formed a plan. She made a beeline for the front door.

If she could do a quick check of the parking lot and the perimeter of the building, she'd be back before Jo could miss her. If the sheriff wasn't outside, she'd have Jo call him. This couldn't wait.

Elizabeth flung the front door outward on its hinges. The door thunked against the wooden siding.

"Easy there, She-Hulk. A few seconds later and you would've knocked me clear out into the gravel."

Ira mounted the steps to the front door, two at a time.

Elizabeth forgot her immediate mission and remembered her original purpose. "I'm glad I almost ran into you," she said. "The auction is about to start. Herodotus was among the first to mention auctions back in 500 BC. But he was selling women, which is a completely different situation."

A smile teased the corner of Ira's mouth. Like a cat that ate the mouse, it was as though he tried but failed to tamp down his mirth. Elizabeth knew she needed to step up her professional game if she wanted to be in business with this man.

He wore a black felt cowboy hat, button down shirt, and a sport coat with his pressed denim. Silver at his buckle, on his shoes, and around his hat band spoke of money. He was a svelte Garth Brooks, presentable and commanding. Here she was, harried and sweating. She considered herself lucky he seemed amused.

"I'm sorry. You just got here, and I'm yammering on like a cockatiel." Elizabeth stepped back from the door, and it swung shut behind her. She reached for the handle again, yanked it open. "There's plenty to eat and drink still. We have chili and this incredible cornbread—"

"Oh, that won't be necessary," Ira said. He reached a hand under his open jacket to pat his stomach. "I've already eaten. I'd love a beer, though. Maybe we could find some time to chat about business, too. Er, if you're up for it."

Elizabeth didn't hear him. Her ears filled with a rushing sound. Like the ocean inside the conch shell she'd held to the side of her head on her honeymoon in Hawaii. Like the trains from the Underground that whooshed by on the platforms in

London during her visit senior year. It was as though every-thing muted as she focused on what she'd seen.

For under Ira's jacket, tucked into his horsehair belt, Eliz-abeth saw the glint of silver, the curve of bone.

"Uh, um. Yeah," she said, a verbal stumble. *Find Clint. Now.* "My brother is inside, with the beer," she added. "Or is it Danny? Someone will serve you. But not me. Don't go any-where. I mean, don't leave until I find you. I'll be right back..." She hooked a thumb over her shoulder but didn't finish the sentence.

Ira gave her an appraising look, as though deciding her current state. He must have found her passable, as with a nod and a touch of his hat brim, he disappeared inside.

Elizabeth ran for the cruiser parked at the side of the lot.

47

EMPTY. ELIZABETH STARED INTO the vacant sheriff's department vehicle for all of ten seconds before spinning on her heel to dash back inside.

The warmth and bustle of the crowd hit her the moment she was back inside. The auction was in full swing, and the masses pressed into the building to take part. Everyone wanted a closer look at auction items. Elizabeth shouldered her way through the crowd, like a salmon swimming upstream.

The auctioneer wielded the microphone with finesse. He was six and half feet of fast-talking cowboy. He could detail a hand-tooled, turquoise-studded handbag at breakneck speed. Even those not planning to bid wanted to hear the man at his work. Volunteers would bring up an item or an envelope stuffed with a gift card, hand the auctioneer a description card, and the man would be off, his words a purr against the hum of the crowd.

Connie Ann, the florist, held one of the donated quilts tight to her chest. She spotted Elizabeth before she could sneak by. "Look what I won! Oh, and hey—Jo was looking for you."

Shoot. There was no time to explain to Jo, but she did need to find Clint. Jo would understand—in the long run. "I'll find her." *One way or another.*

"He's great, isn't he?" Connie Ann nudged toward the auctioneer with her shoulder. "Like a train engine, picking up steam."

"Auctioneers can say about two hundred fifty words a minute. Imagine if trains could talk. Excuse me, I've got to go find—Jo."

The hall was both bigger and smaller when chock full of people. The opposite end appeared so far away yet there was hardly room to move.

On her way through the crowd, Elizabeth overheard snatches of conversations.

"Reynolds donated the three-night stay at Bar Eight. Show off."

"I'm bidding on the log cabin quilt. I've had the pieces for one of my own in my basket for months. You know how that goes."

"Absolutely not, you do not need a second piece of cake!"

"We need to get the kids to bed. Beat the crowd."

"Laney would have loved this."

At this last comment, Elizabeth slowed.

Two women stood in front of the picture from the past. It was the same one Elizabeth had studied, in which a hopeful crew celebrated a new roof on Kearney Hall.

"She would have. This is the stuff she lived for, people getting together. Community."

"...pressed them to make this happen, you know. Get this place up and going again. Those bullheaded, selfish apes."

"They weren't all bad. I mean one brother was decent. And the other guy was quiet. Laney was the real CEO, in a way..."

The other guy?

"I do kind of wonder if it came from guilt. At first, you know?" This woman wore a bolo tie atop a faded navy shirt. Silver earrings in the shape of feathers dangled from her lobes.

Elizabeth tried to catch the woman's reaction. She saw a slight shrug, the woman's brows drawing together.

"Like it or not, she made it rich in the dotcom era when it was about crushing everyone you could. Got to sleep at night with that over your head."

"At least she cashed in. Got out of there before the crash." The earrings danced when the speaker shook her head.

"I heard it was for Wallace's sake. Sure complicated their retirement."

"And look, now everything is his. Wonder what he'll do with it."

"I wonder if he'll stay single." The woman winked at her friend.

Elizabeth moved on. A recent death distilled down to the sudden availability of husband material was awkward gossip to hear.

Outside the window, near the woodshed, she spotted Deputy Ryland in tight communication with a Game and Fish warden. Heads together, they were deep in conversation. She pressed her way to the edge of the room and ducked out the door.

Stars winked into place as purple inked into the twilight. Bats zipped across the sky. A cow lowed from a nearby pasture as Elizabeth jogged her way over to the duo. She interrupted, breathless.

"There's a second gun!"

48

"YOU'RE GOING TO NEED to start from the beginning."

Elizabeth shook her head, wild-eyed. "There isn't time. Ira has it. It's on him now. I saw it!"

"Ira?" Ryland frowned. The name was unfamiliar to the young deputy.

"He's waving a gun at people?" The other officer's voice was cold and clear.

Elizabeth squeezed her hands into brief fists, then released them. "No. He has a gun. In his belt. Right now."

"Elizabeth," Ryland started. The other officer cleared his throat, and the deputy restarted. "Excuse me, Ms. Blau. It's not illegal to carry a gun here."

"But it's under his jacket. Why hide it?"

The other officer cleared his throat again. "To be frank, ma'am, half the people in that place could be carrying. Don't even need a permit, and we can't fleece them for it. Check one, we'd have to check them all. That'd go over like a fart in church."

Elizabeth pleaded with the lawmen. "You don't understand. It's the same gun." She turned to Ryland. "It matches the one at George's house."

"Impossible."

"I'm telling you, I saw it."

"We have that weapon, Ms. Blau. We confiscated it as the murder weapon."

"What do you mean?"

"It's in our evidence lock up, as we speak. We don't give back murder weapons, even if their owners have an ironclad alibi."

"But did you look in the box?"

"We see a great many guns, ma'am. And the boxes that carry them."

Elizabeth stamped in frustration. Guy's box, the one she'd seen him open the first day they'd met, two velvet divots for matching, silver pistols. Like heirlooms. "At least say you'll keep an eye on him."

Ryland addressed her. "Ms. Blau, we are investigating the death of Guy Henderson. We're doing all we can with what we know, I assure you."

"And Laney? What about her case?"

"We've got every iron in the fire."

Unsatisfied, Elizabeth looked from Ryland to the other officer, doubtful. "Did you find the chain?"

Ryland frowned at her. He puffed out his cheeks, then turned to his colleague. "Ms. Blau found the ring in question." To Elizabeth, he said, "Sheriff will release all public information when he is able."

Elizabeth took the hint. "I see. Thank you, *Deputy*." She drew out Ryland's title with a hint of mockery.

The other officer nodded in a polite dismissal, and the men moved off as a hint.

The moon shone silver beams into the twilight. Elizabeth stood in the side yard, hands on her hips. Snippets of the auctioneer leaked from the cracked windows. A puff of smoke escaped the chimney. The scent of burning pine followed on the evening air. Constellations surfaced in the twilight.

Elizabeth considered the pieces she held. A family business. Jealousy, lies, and secrets, some bought and paid for. Elizabeth had more questions and she needed answers. Ira was there and he had a pistol from a matching set, the other of which was used to murder Guy Henderson.

"Our next item up for bid is a brand new Gibson banjo, signed by none other than Rob McCoury. Bidding will start at two hundred dollars."

Elizabeth knew where to find Kade.

49

K ADE HELD HIS BANDANA-COVERED fan at chin height, ready to pounce from the front row.

"Can I get five hundred?" Paddles went up around the room. "I got five hundred. Six, can I get six hundred? Six hundred, thank you. Do we have seven hundred?"

The auctioneer flowed with the crowd. Bids escalated to one thousand and then higher. Elizabeth nudged her way forward.

Kade's face was alert, his shoulders tense. He rocked onto the balls of his feet as though he may need to spring onto the stage at any moment.

"Two thousand, can I get two thousand dollars?" The auctioneer paused to scan the room. The woman with whom Kade had traded the last few bids gave him a little bow. She lowered her paddle so that Kade's was the sole bandana raised. "Four thousand going once..."

In moments, the banjo was Kade's. Elizabeth tailed him on his way toward the payment tables.

"Kade. Kade, hold up."

Elizabeth stepped in front of him. Sadness flashed across his face, then irritation. *I may deserve some of that.*

"I have a banjo to buy," he said, gesturing to the tables. "Can it wait a minute?"

"No. I mean, it will only take a minute."

He regarded her there, in the middle of what had earlier served as the dance floor. "Okay."

"George isn't your real uncle, is he? I mean, your biological uncle."

Kade flinched as though she'd slapped him. "How did you....? But I never—"

"It started with the blond hair, to be fair. But it was something Guy said. He called George his partner. Then the fact that your father lived in a huge house. It just didn't add up."

They'd reached the payment table. Kade held out his paddle and pointed to the instrument. "Stepbrothers. My grandfather married George's mom and there was a prenup. Guy ponied up the seed money for the business, which was why he controlled the assets. Doesn't matter, though. George was more family to me than my own father. Laney, too." He signed the auction slip, then reached into his back pocket. "Mom said sometimes we get to choose our family, and I never questioned that. Not in my situation." Kade patted at his other pockets. "Excuse me," he said to the cashier. "I think I left my wallet in my truck. I'll be right back. Scout's honor."

Elizabeth offered the cashier an awkward smile as Kade ducked out the door. She needed to think, and a live auction wasn't the best place to focus.

"You sure he's coming back?" The woman tapped her long nails on the tabletop, doubtful.

"Of course he is. He inherited a bunch of cash. Well, not a bunch. His dad died."

Another quilt sold, and Elizabeth checked her watch. "I'll go get him."

The woman called after her. "The item goes back up for bid if you don't pay for it!"

Elizabeth ducked out the side door as she stepped into the cooler night air and rounded the building.

Where did Kade park? His truck wasn't in the main lot outside the hall. It must be along the road. Elizabeth debated whether to hoof it over to the highway to look or wait for him back on the porch. A coyote howled at the moon, a bright crescent in the deepening sky.

A movement caught her eye. On the front porch, someone slipped around the edge. She saw a flash of movement between the bales of hay stacked on the porch. The person snuck around first one, then the other, and then hid behind a pillar.

She recognized the hat. *Ira.*

He'd nestled himself between two bales. Elizabeth, in the shadows beyond the porch, was unseen. She watched him scan the road. There was a brief chirp from an armed alarm, a flash of headlights.

A glint of silver caught the moonlight next to the bale, and Elizabeth gasped.

Ira had slipped the barrel of the pistol between the bales. He eased off the safety. Heard Kade's whistle as he approached, no doubt with wallet in hand.

Elizabeth had no time to think, only the briefest moment to act. She dove for the nearest stack of bales near where Ira lay in wait. With a hard shove, she toppled the stack, sending the bales crashing down on top of Ira. He yelped and the gun went off.

Kade fell to the ground.

50

W HEN THE BALES FELL, there was a sickening snap followed by a moan from behind the wreckage. She didn't stop to check on Ira but ran for Kade.

Kade clutched at his shoulder as blood seeped from between his fingers. His face contorted into a display of pain. He lay in the fetal position as beads of sweat crossed his brow.

"I'll get you help, Kade. Stay here and breathe."

Feet pounded out of the Hall doors and across the driveway, shouts and yells behind them. Ryland skidded onto the sandy surface and dropped to his knees next to her.

"Where was he shot?"

"Shoulder." Kade groaned, then added, "Or arm. The whole area is on fire, and I can't tell."

"I'll call 911," Elizabeth said. She was lightheaded from the sight of red leeching into Kade's flannel.

"Already on their way," Ryland said. "There's a medical kit in the closet inside. Can you get that? Then let's find out if anyone here is a nurse or a doctor."

"But Ira is on the porch," Elizabeth said.

"Officer Decker has him. Go!"

Elizabeth heard Ryland talking to Kade, no doubt to soothe and distract. "Too early to tell if you'll have to sit out softball season. Wouldn't be a bad thing for my team, though."

Elizabeth pushed her way toward the hall. People were streaming out of the doors, and she fought to get inside. Several of those gathered outside had guns in hand. The officer—Decker— had been right.

Elizabeth collided with Jo in the hallway.

"What happened? Who got shot?"

"Kade," Elizabeth said. "But just in the arm. Or shoulder. I didn't stop to look." The reality of a bullet passing through her boyfriend's flesh made her queasy. She pushed the thought out of her mind. "It was a gun. The same one that I saw."

"Sheriff dropped Rhett and Benny off with Marj since it was getting late. He's safe." Jo reached into the hall closet and grabbed the first aid kit. "My idea, so we'd be free to clean. Get mad at me later. Clint should be back here any minute."

When they got to Kade, another man was kneeling next to him. He pressed a wad of fabric to Kade's arm. Ryland ripped the sleeve off his own shirt and folded it into a makeshift gauze. Ryland had propped Kade up by wadding up his government issued jacket and placing it behind his neck.

Jo handed over the pack. The assistant, a Sheridan veterinarian, dug into the medical supplies. While he went to work, Elizabeth and Jo got out of the way and watched from the edge of the tight circle.

Elizabeth's chest constricted and she willed the blood to stop.

51

THE VETERINARIAN HAD SLOWED his work, having cleaned and prepped the wound as best he could. "How long until the ambulance gets here?"

"Shouldn't be more than another ten minutes." Ryland was grim, steady.

The veterinarian nodded and left to clean up. Elizabeth again squatted down by Kade and held his hand.

"I was worried there," she said.

"Doc fixed me right up," Kade said. "As good a field dress as one could ask for, given that I'm not four-legged ranch stock. I should heal right as rain. What did it look like?"

"What are you talking about?"

"The gun," Kade said. "Describe it to me."

Elizabeth thought of Ira, captured on the porch. "Well, it had a long silver barrel. Shiny, like it had been polished. And a pale handle. Bone. Carved. It's the exact one I saw in George's hands at the open house."

"There are two," Kade said. He inhaled and exhaled a breath, a slow release of the pain. "I found the other one in Guy's safety deposit box. He had so many, I didn't think anything of it."

"But Ira would have known about both."

Ryland was dubious. "How do you know that?"

"He worked for them for decades, just like Laney. He knew their finances inside and out. My guess is he kept stock of Guy's belongings because he would have had to insure his place for him. And he could've found the matching pistol at

George's when he was trying to sell the house. He would have had keys to both places."

Ryland interrupted. "But how can we know the guns were switched if they're exactly the same?"

Sirens sounded in the distance, growing louder.

"I know how," Elizabeth said. "The one from the safety deposit box won't have Guy's prints on it, but the one you confiscated will."

52

"THEY BOOKED HIM FOR reckless discharge of a firearm. My guess is he will lawyer up but not before they up that charge."

"To murder or embezzlement?"

That morning, Elizabeth had set Rhett down inside the Wolfs' house, planted a kiss on his forehead, and he was off and running. Jo had pressured Clint into becoming foster parents for kittens, and the latest box of fur balls were among Rhett's favorites. Jo kept them in a huge, triple-decker crate in her laundry room. It was warm and snug, and she could keep a gate up so the golden retrievers wouldn't over-love their tiny guests. She guessed Rhett beelined back there with his new furry friends.

"My guess is a mix of both. If he actually has any of that company money left, he'll need it to pay the lawyers' fees."

"What did they find out about Laney?"

Jo peeked to make sure Rhett was out of earshot. "He confessed when they showed him the necklace chain. Didn't even get to the needle. Said she planned to expose him if he didn't come clean. Guy would have sued the pants off Ira and he knew it."

Elizabeth remembered the notebooks. "Kade found Laney's notes. Guy hired her to help him get his affairs in order. She'd been matching his assets to insurance policies. If Ira had known she'd documented all he's stolen, he would've torched that building along with the house. But why frame George?"

"George would look like the bitter brother, the one who was shut out of the deal, come back from prison to get revenge." Jo shook her head, disbelieving. "My heart goes out to Wallace. That man has gone through too much."

Elizabeth was silent. There were no words of comfort, only loss for Wallace Horowitz.

"How is Kade doing?"

Elizabeth had visited Kade every day since the incident. She'd brought dinner, taken over barn chores, and otherwise tried to be helpful. They watched a marathon of Clint Eastwood movies, gorged on popcorn. It would be akin to summer camp if it weren't based on tragedy.

Thanks to the quick and clean work of the veterinarian, Kade was healing. Another few days and he would be off the pain medication, a requirement to returning to his shop and the heavy machinery. Until then, Raj, back from his fishing trip, and Alma worked overtime so their boss could rest. They promised Elizabeth everything would run fine and charged her to keep their favorite boss off his feet as long as possible. It was hard for Kade to stay put, let alone not work.

"He is a bit stir crazy," Elizabeth said, "but feeling better by the minute. Won't be long now before he's pounding fenders and taking names. In fact, I'm picking him up to take him to George's house for dinner."

They pulled up to the now familiar snug cabin along the creek.

Brutus and Leia bounded from the hatchback and into the yard where they wrestled and tumbled among the leaves, joyful at their freedom from the cramped ride. Elizabeth extracted Rhett from his car seat while Benny released himself from the booster. Kade stood and stretched his good arm before clutching at his injured shoulder.

"You good?"

Kade watched the boys and dogs romping in the yard. "Yeah," he said "I'm good. Real good."

He wrapped his arm around her shoulder as they walked toward the front door. Elizabeth had a black bottom pie in her hands. Chocolate shavings, curled in half loops, trembled with her steps. A soft, autumnal breeze teased at the fine hair sticking out from underneath her beanie. She'd donned a waffle weave henley and topped it with a vest. The nights were getting colder, and she knew what was coming. Fall was her favorite, and it was fleeting.

A blanket of yellow aspen leaves dried among the pine needles. Like weightless, golden coins, they fluttered on the breeze. A curl of smoke escaped the chimney.

Before they had a chance to knock, the door opened. The heady scent of roasted pumpkin, cinnamon, and nutmeg greeted them, along with George in his apron.

"My favorite dinner guests," he said. "Come in. I put a log on the fire and the soup is almost ready."

As Elizabeth followed Kade inside the now familiar house, boys and dogs squeezed in between, and she allowed herself a sincere and humble moment of thanksgiving.

53

ELIZABETH'S PHONE GAVE HER driving orders through the speaker. She glanced into the rearview mirror. Rhett squirmed in his carseat. He clutched a plastic sheep, walking it along the door. "Almost there, buddy."

Just past the house with the sweet woman and the daredevil dog, Jack, Elizabeth pulled her car off to the side of the road.

She zipped her jacket over her sweater and opened the passenger side door. Leia hopped out and sniffed their surroundings. Elizabeth reached in to free Rhett from his carseat and bundle him into a coat.

When she backed out of the car, she set him on the ground and took his hand. As they walked past a sign hanging from a wooden post, Elizabeth watched her son take in the scenery.

The leaves were all but gone from the deciduous trees, but the conifers held court in green. Birds called to each other over the nearby burble of water.

Elizabeth picked her way through the brush with Rhett. When they came to a big stump or rock, she would take both of Rhett's hands in her own to lift him up and over the barrier.

At the stream, a collection of chickadees cheeped from bare aspen branches. A squirrel skittered up and across a trunk, a wad of dry leaves in its mouth.

Elizabeth looked back at the For Sale sign, wedged into the shoulder of the road.

A dozen feet farther and they were at the edge of a little stream. A bank of pebbles, water like crystal. She flipped her scarf an extra loop around her neck and crouched down to Rhett's height.

"I'm going to do big things," she said to her son. "For you, for me. Whether this plot of land or another one, I'm going to get us a place. A home. Somewhere you will always be welcome. You'll see, you're going to be proud of your mama."

Rhett looked up at her, his earnest face trusting, eyes full of love. Her sweet boy leaned in for a hug and whispered, "Mama."

* * *

Read the Series!

Thanks for being a reader.

Want to find out when Erin's next books will be out?

Subscribe her newsletter, get a free copy of *The Sheriff's Wife,* and more at erinlark.com

The Sheridan County Mysteries

The Sheriff's Wife(prequel)

The New Teacher(#1)

The Sled Dog(#2)

The Dead Swede(#3)

The Master Mechanic (#4)

The Banjo Player (#5)

Reviews help readers find books they'll enjoy and authors find people who love their stories.

Please consider leaving a review on your favorite bookshop's website or with Goodreads.

About Erin

From the desert southwest, Erin fell in love with Sheridan County on the banks of Piney Creek. An award-winning science teacher, avid archer, and hack watercolorist, she lives for the outdoors. Erin and her family divide their time between Wyoming, Washington, and Arizona because life is too short to play favorites.

Appreciation

This story, like the first in the series, was inspired by the musicians who meet each week at the Occidental Hotel in Buffalo, Wyoming to showcase their talents and connect a community with songs from yesterday and today. If you find yourself in the town that inspired other books such as the Longmire series, I hope you'll stop by this incredible building and have a look around for yourself.

Three cheers for the Board of Directors of Kearney Community Hall for breathing new life into such a beloved historical building near Story. I appreciate the patient tours, frequent updates, and the answers to my endless questions. May the halls ring with good cheer for decades to come.

As always, the attention and detail of my editor Paula Lester is greatly appreciated.

Terrilani Chong continues to be my first and treasured reader and for that I am deeply grateful.

Last, but never least, all my love to Bryan and Ava for being my biggest fans.